W9-BTM-988

"I want you, Chloe. Come up to my room."

She blinked up at him. Wanton lust made his blue eyes black as the night surrounding them. She saw her face reflected in his eyes. Her lips swollen, her face flushed, her brown eyes opened wide with pleasure. The desire in her eyes mirrored his.

"Yes," she murmured huskily. She didn't know what she was doing—and she didn't care. She only knew she ached for the man holding her in his arms, the man whose kisses caused her heart to race and her blood to heat.

He kissed her again with urgent, demanding, possessive lips. She responded eagerly, meeting each kiss with equal fervor, entangling her fingers in his hair and arching her neck as he showered a hot trail of kisses up and down its slender length.

"Why not right here?" she murmured brazenly. "I don't think I can wait until your room."

He grinned at her. Straight, white, beautiful teeth flashed in the darkness.

"What a bold suggestion from a maiden fairy."

She smiled languidly at his teasing. "Who said I was a maiden fairy?"

He chuckled. "I'm glad I came to this party."

Chloe fluttered her eyelashes. "Because of me?"

Max's hot, appreciative stare made Chloe flush. "Most definitely because of you."

Courting His Royal Highness

by

Amy Hahn

This is a work of fiction. Names, characters, places, and incidents are either the product of the author's imagination or are used fictitiously, and any resemblance to actual persons living or dead, business establishments, events, or locales, is entirely coincidental.

Courting His Royal Highness

COPYRIGHT © 2008 by Amy Hahn

All rights reserved. No part of this book may be used or reproduced in any manner whatsoever without written permission of the author or The Wild Rose Press except in the case of brief quotations embodied in critical articles or reviews.
Contact Information: info@thewildrosepress.com

Cover Art by *Angela Anderson*

The Wild Rose Press
PO Box 706
Adams Basin, NY 14410-0706
Visit us at www.thewildrosepress.com

Publishing History
First Champagne Rose Edition, 2008
Print ISBN 1-60154-378-6

Published in the United States of America

Dedication

For my husband, Chris.
No words can express my appreciation
for your friendship, love, selfless support
and unfaltering belief in me.
I'm a lucky girl.

Chapter One

She was going to be famous, a household name all over America and across the world. Yes, she, Chloe Tanner from rural Minnesota, was about to take her very first step into stardom—and she could barely contain her excitement.

Last week she had been a twenty-five-year-old nothing. In fact, right now she was still a nobody, at least to anyone except her loving family and small group of close friends. But in a month that would all change drastically. Why? Because she was going to become a TV star. The EVE network, a women-focused cable channel, had selected *her* to be the hostess of its newest reality show, *Courting His Royal Highness*.

Chloe could hardly believe her luck. Thousands had auditioned for the role of the hostess, but the producers of the show and executives at EVE had chosen her over all those other knockouts. Her arm was bruised black and blue from pinching herself two times a day for the last week to make sure she truly wasn't dreaming.

But she wasn't dreaming. The limo she currently rode in was proof of that, along with the new wardrobe EVE had outfitted her with, and the special invitation she'd received to the network's annual Halloween Masquerade Ball.

Chloe glanced at the invitation in her hand. She traced the scrawling words with the tip of one finger. It was a beautiful invitation: the background paper a brilliant purple, the letters a glittering silver; a witch flew on her broomstick across a full moon, and

1

a spider web decorated each corner.

She still couldn't believe it. Yep, she was headed for the big time. Finally, after years of disappointment and rejection, which did wonders to a girl's self-esteem. But she never gave up. She'd always believed in her dream, and now she was about to step out of the shadows of obscurity into the glorious Hollywood limelight.

A girlish giggle erupted from her perfectly painted lips. She covered her mouth in embarrassment and looked up at the driver. He didn't seem to notice, focused on driving through the myriad of L.A. traffic. She breathed a sigh of relief and relaxed against the leather upholstery.

Nervous butterflies fluttered in her stomach. She hadn't been able to eat a thing all day. The very idea of hobnobbing with the rich and famous had her in a tailspin.

Chloe turned her head and looked out the window. The historic Hollywood Boulevard was loaded with people. On a Saturday night in early October, the Boulevard was busier than usual. It still wasn't the safest or cleanest part of town, but big steps were being made to improve it. Still, tourists were often shocked to find how truly unglamorous this famous stretch was.

She smiled, recalling her first visit to Grauman's Chinese Theater. Oh, how thrilling it had been to place her hands on the imprints of Marilyn Monroe's. The place still held magic—that classic Hollywood magic—and tourists from all over the world eagerly flocked there in hopes of experiencing it.

"We're almost there, Miss Tanner."

"Thank you, Sam."

The driver smiled at her in the rearview mirror. "Have a good time tonight."

She grinned. "I know I will."

"I'll be back to pick you up around midnight."

"Sounds great."

"Are you sure you want to picked up that early? These Hollywood shindigs usually tend to last into the wee hours of the morning."

"I'd like to get some sleep; after all, my first day on the job is tomorrow. I don't quite understand the weekend start, but they call the shots."

Sam smiled. "Yes, they do, Miss Tanner."

He pulled the sleek black car up in front of the Hollywood Roosevelt. The hotel towered twelve floors over Hollywood Boulevard. During Hollywood's golden era, it had been a favorite of movie royalty, and many claimed it was haunted—which made it the perfect spot for tonight's Halloween extravaganza.

Chloe reached for the door but then remembered Sam would open it for her. She wasn't sure if she would ever get used to being pampered. She was accustomed to doing things by her lonesome—she depended on no one but herself. Other people simply disappointed her. Except for a few close friends—only a handful—and her family, she didn't trust a single soul. She had been burned too many times.

Sam opened her door and offered her his arm; she took it and placed one trembling foot onto the pavement. It was lined with Hollywood stars. She wondered if she would ever be among them.

"Good evening, Miss Tanner." Sam touched the brim of his cap. "Is there anything else I can do for you?"

"No, Sam, I think I'll be just fine."

Sam nodded. He closed the door and walked over to the driver's door.

Chloe's heart lurched. She stared up at the massive hotel. Was she ready for this? She didn't think so. Maybe she should get back in the limo and tell Sam to drive her back to her tiny apartment.

"You look beautiful."

Chloe blinked and glanced over at Sam. He offered a kind smile. He was a decent guy. You didn't meet too many of those in Los Angeles.

"Flattery will get you everywhere."

He laughed. "I'm hopeful, but I doubt it." He waved. "Enjoy."

She blew him her best Marilyn Monroe kiss. He chuckled before slamming the door shut and driving away.

Chloe watched the limo until it disappeared from sight. The butterflies continued to dance excitedly in her belly. She clutched the invitation tightly and moved towards the front doors.

"Hello, pretty lady, welcome to the Roosevelt Hotel."

A tremulous smile spread her lips as the doorman opened up the door for her and swept her inside.

His eyes twinkled at her attire.

"I'm assuming you're here for the EVE Halloween Ball?"

She nodded and showed him the invitation.

"Nice costume."

"Thanks."

She saw her reflection in one of the many mirrors in the hotel's elegant lobby. She was dressed as Mab, Queen of the Fairies. Although she'd had no choice in the matter—the EVE executives had sent over the costume—she had to admit she looked rather spectacular in it. Her midnight hair tumbled down about her shoulders. A light sprinkling of imitation fairy dust made the dark tresses sparkle. The gown was made of silk, a rich, vibrant red. It looked fantastic against her pale skin and complimented her black hair. A tiara of fake rubies and diamonds crowned her head, and a matching necklace circled her neck. The sandals decorating her size 8 feet were nearly invisible, the straps forming a web-like pattern across her feet made of a sheer gossamer fabric. Iridescent wings completed the ensemble.

The doorman directed her to the room where the ball was being held. She thanked him, gave him a generous tip, and slowly walked through the lobby where other partygoers lingered. Witches and vampires sprawled across the brocade couches. A cowboy and cowgirl were in a deep embrace. And Cruella De Vil and the evil queen from Snow White appeared to be arguing about something.

Chloe flashed her invitation to the skeleton at the ballroom door. He bowed and gestured her inside.

This was it. This was her chance to network and advance her career. She took a deep breath and stepped inside.

It didn't take her long to find Mr. Carridine, her new boss, and his entourage, dressed as the beloved characters from *The Wizard of Oz*. She exchanged small talk with them before heading to the bar.

"A white wine, please. Chardonnay," she ordered. The drinks were free, and she was certainly happy about that—she only had about ten dollars to her name.

The bartender gently set a large wine goblet in front of her, a souvenir glass with the words *EVE's Halloween Masquerade Ball* emblazoned across the surface.

Chloe took a sip. The liquid, slightly flavored with apples, felt deliciously refreshing rushing down her throat. No red wine for her. White was the only way to go.

"A lovely woman like you shouldn't be drinking alone."

Chloe jumped at the sound of the deep, masculine voice. She turned to find herself gazing into a pair of magnetic eyes, eyes so incredibly blue they put the sky to shame.

"Is this seat taken?"

She shook her head, unable to mouth a single word. The man was incredibly handsome. He looked to be in his mid-thirties, with hair as dark as her own and a lazy smile that sent shock waves throughout her entire system.

"So, who are you supposed to be?" he inquired after ordering a martini—shaken, not stirred. "Let me guess." He studied her for a minute or two with his amazing blue eyes, and then snapped his fingers. "I've got it. You're a fairy."

Chloe blushed under his intense gaze as she finished off the remainder of her wine. "Close enough. Did the wings give me away?"

He laughed. She couldn't resist smiling. She liked the sound of his laughter—rich and vibrant and full of life. Here was a guy who knew not to take life too seriously.

"Would you like another wine, my fairy princess?"

"Fairy queen," she corrected with a giggle. "And, yes, I would enjoy another glass."

He smiled again.

Chloe's heart thumped wildly in her breast. Gosh, he was altogether yummy. And he had dimples. Chloe loved a man with dimples. She happened to have a soft spot for blue eyes, too. He also had an accent, but she couldn't place it. It was subtle, but it vibrated in his baritone voice, signaling quite clearly that he had not spent his entire life in America.

"Okay, so what or who are you?"

"Bond. James Bond." He popped the martini olive into his mouth with a lopsided grin.

Yep, he was adorable. Desire flamed inside Chloe, and its intensity startled her. She had just met the guy, for goodness sake! She wasn't the type of girl to sleep with a complete stranger. But he was so hunky. He filled out the black tux to perfection—better than Sean Connery, Roger Moore, Pierce Brosnan, or Daniel Craig.

"Nice to meet you, James."

He shook her outstretched hand. "Glad to me you, too, fairy queen."

His touch was electric. Tentacles of heat webbed up her arm. "Mab, Queen of the Fairies."

"Ah, yes, the fairy queen of Celtic legends. Shakespeare made her famous by referencing her in Romeo and Juliet. A tragic tale."

"Yes," she agreed. She loved Shakespeare, especially his love sonnets—she was a helpless romantic at heart. Her family and friends found great humor in the fact she still stubbornly believed in happy endings and true love. Didn't every girl? The last few years had tested her beliefs, but she refused to get too pessimistic. And now she had no reason to be. Her fairy tale ending was right around the corner. Minus the guy. At least for the moment.

"I'm very happy to meet you, Mab."

His fingers still touched hers, his skin warm and smooth. Shivers ran up and down her arm. She wondered what it would be like to feel his fingertips caress her breasts. Then she drew her hand away, startled by the erotic thought. Her wine arrived, and she quickly focused her attention on downing a few more drops of the cool liquid.

"Spectacular party."

She agreed. The entire ballroom was decked out in Halloween decor. Purple tablecloths decorated the long tables, black lace draped the chairs, and glowing jack-o-lanterns grinned as toothless centerpieces. The food even had a Halloween theme. The menu listed Slime Salad, Pumpkin Soup, Dracula's Pasta, and Frankenstein Cake. The band, dressed in gothic garb, currently entertained everyone with its version of Frank Sinatra's *Black Magic*.

"Sampled the food yet?"

He shook his head. "You?"

"No." Her stomach rumbled. She gave it a pat.

He wiggled his eyebrows at her. "I guess your stomach has something to say about that."

She groaned. "You heard that?"

"Sure did."

Chloe felt her cheeks flush.

The bartender pointed at her empty glass. "Another?"

"Yes, please."

He filled her wineglass.

James Bond raised an eyebrow at her. "That's your third glass."

She shrugged as she took a sip. He made her nervous. She didn't know what else to do but drink. "Got a problem with that?" she asked.

He held up a hand. "Not at all. I just don't want Queen Mab to get ill."

She giggled. Wine spewed from her mouth. She slapped a black and orange napkin against her lips. And hiccuped rather loudly.

He grinned. His grin was just as adorable as his smile, and Chloe felt the urge to kiss him. In fact, she wanted to do more than kiss him. She wanted to throw herself against him, strip away his James Bond tux, and make mad, passionate love to him.

Yikes! Perhaps she shouldn't have had three glasses of alcohol on an empty stomach. Bad idea. Horrible idea. Idiotic idea. But it was too late to go back now. The damage was done. Chloe felt lightheaded—tipsiness had begun.

She needed to get away from him. She lost control when she drank wine. She seldom drank, but when she did, her body had zero tolerance. Zippo.

Egad, what had she been thinking? How could she get drunk at her first big Hollywood party? She needed to get away from hottie James Bond before she did something she really regretted.

"It was nice meeting you," she whispered.

"Hey, take it easy." He steadied her with one hand as she wobbled on her feet. "Are you staying at the hotel? I could escort you back to your room."

The room tilted. She lost her balance and fell against him. He smelled good. He smelled clean, of soap and shampoo and cologne she didn't recognize. His chest was strong and broad, and she could feel his heart beating beneath her fingertips.

"Perhaps you need some air."

She agreed. "And food. I haven't eaten anything all day."

He looked down into her upturned face with his wide blue eyes. "No wonder you're teetering on your feet. Let me help you. We'll go sit by the pool and have some food brought out."

Chloe didn't argue. She let him guide her through the crowded ballroom, clinging to his arm with her gaze on the floor. She didn't want anyone to see her like this. It was mortifying. She only hoped some food would help balance the flood of fermented drink flowing through her starved body.

She gratefully gulped in the cool night air as they stepped out into the pool area. The chlorinated water beckoned. For a second, she seriously contemplated throwing off her clothes and diving in.

"Feel better?"

"Yeah, I think so." Chloe sat down on one of the poolside chairs. "You don't really have to stay with me."

"I insist." He sat down beside her and draped one strong arm around her. "It would be ungentlemanly of me to leave a woman all by herself."

9

She glanced around and was surprised to find they were alone. She was surpised no one else was enjoying the beautiful evening. She raised an eyebrow. "Oh? Trying to save me?" she teased.

"I'm feeling in character."

"Well, I don't need saving, Mr. Bond."

"So, you're the independent type."

Chloe raised her chin. "Yep."

He tweaked the end of her nose. "Well, I'd like to try."

Her heart stopped beating and dropped to her toes. The man was flirting with her. A James Bond lookalike with sky-blue eyes and a heavenly smile and gorgeous laugh and muscular body was actually flirting with *her*, Chloe Tanner, a Midwestern farm girl. Unbelievable. Her luck really had changed.

The food arrived, and she happily grabbed her plate. Her stomach growled so loudly that she thought she would die from embarrassment.

"Did you know Marilyn Monroe posed for an ad for suntan lotion on that diving board?"

The debonair British spy, complete with foreign accent, followed her line of sight. "I didn't know that. Fascinating."

"And did you also know her ghost haunts the mirror next to the elevators?" She loved Hollywood trivia. Her friends sometimes called her obsessed, due to the amount of celebrity and movie magazines she subscribed to. It was her little hobby, besides yoga and snorkeling.

His blue eyes met hers. "You are full of interesting trivia."

"Do you know anything about your character?" She gestured to his attire before filling her mouth with a spoon overflowing with Dracula pasta. She could eat a boatload, but she didn't want to scare him away. She noticed he wasn't eating a thing.

"I do own the James Bond DVD collection;

however, I admit I am not a film fanatic."

She swallowed the pasta and piled another spoonful full. "Are you calling me crazy?"

"Most certainly not. I don't have a whole lot of time to watch movies."

She gaped at him. "Everyone loves movies."

He shrugged. His hand rested along the side of her thigh. She could feel the burn of his skin through the thin fabric of her gown. She hoped he liked black lace underwear. Jeez, what was she thinking? She had known this guy a total of twenty minutes, and already she couldn't wait to jump into bed with him. But who wouldn't want to go to bed with James Bond? Every man wanted to be him. Every woman wanted to be with him—and not in the purely platonic way.

"In my line of work, I don't have too much free time."

She chewed the last of her pasta and took a generous gulp of water. "What do you do?"

He shook his head and placed two fingers against her lips. "Not now. Not yet."

Boy, he was secretive. Exactly like James Bond. She began to wonder if this man really thought he was the guy with a license to kill.

Her lips tingled from his touch. She tried to concentrate on the food. It was delicious. Only the best for EVE's famous Halloween Ball.

"Okay, so what's your real name?"

"Just call me Max."

"Okay, Max, nice to meet you."

"And your name, my queen?"

She gazed into his blue eyes and melted. No way was she leaving the party without some lovin' from this man. Her friends would kill her if she let him slip through her fingers. She could fulfill every woman's fantasy—a daunting task. But someone had to do it.

"Chloe."

His cheeks dimpled for her in the moonlight. "A classic name."

She wrinkled her nose. "It was my grandmother's. I never liked it."

"I think it suits you. A beautiful name for a beautiful woman."

Her cheeks flamed. Heck, she felt as though her entire face blazed fire-engine red. He was a flatterer. Big time. And she rather liked it—it was nice to be complimented.

"Nice to meet you, Chloe."

"And you, Max."

They shook hands again. Her skin sizzled. She couldn't remember the last time a man had affected her so. It was thrilling and just a tad bit scary.

Music drifted out through the open windows and doors, enveloping them in a dreamy melody. It was big band music. Just the type Chloe loved.

"Care to dance with me?"

Her eyes widened. "I'd love to, but I have to warn you I'm not a very good dancer."

Max pulled her onto her feet. "Well, I happen to be a pro."

She rolled her eyes. "Aren't we cocky."

"I only speak the truth."

He lowered his face. She could feel his breath against her cheek, scented with alcohol and spices. Scrumptious. Her legs turned to spaghetti. She leaned against him heavily, very afraid her knees would give out. He cupped her hand in his, and she rested the other on his shoulder. His fingers lightly touched the small of her back as he guided her around the rectangular pool in a spine-tingling waltz, which made her dizzier than the three glasses of wine she had gulped down.

He definitely spoke the truth: he was a spectacular dancer. He belonged in a ballroom. He

12

belonged in a tux. He possessed an arrogance and demeanor that suggested he lived an affluent lifestyle, James Bond or not. Maybe he was a super spy; right now, she didn't care. She only wished to enjoy the moment. Being held in his arms, so close to his body, made her breathless. The fragrance of his cologne wrapped her in a romantic cocoon. For a moment, she became a glamorous movie star from Hollywood's golden age, dancing with her handsome leading man underneath the moon and stars and the historic Roosevelt Hotel.

The song ended. He pulled her close beneath a palm tree. She wrapped her arms about his neck and tilted her head back so she could look up into his handsome face. Her hair cascaded over his arm, and the annoying fairy wings hit her head. Her heart thundered wildly in her breast; he was going to kiss her. She was sure of it. Her woman's instinct told her so.

Max lowered his head over hers, and Chloe closed her eyes in response. His lips brushed against hers, lightly and tenderly. She sighed into his mouth, and the kiss deepened. Then he dragged her up against his tall frame until her hips grazed his groin. Feeling the hardness of his arousal, she gasped. As his tongue plunged into the moist cave of her mouth, Chloe responded hungrily and held him tightly. In her belly, the spark of desire he'd ignited flamed into a fire out of control.

"I want you," he whispered into the sensitive tunnel of her ear.

She shivered and groaned. While his teeth nibbled on her earlobe, the tip of his tongue traced the curve of her ear. "We just met," she whispered, curling her body closer alongside his, his erection hard against her middle.

Max's hands entwined in the tresses of her long hair. "I want you, Chloe. Come up to my room."

She blinked up at him. Wanton lust made his blue eyes black as the night surrounding them. She saw her face reflected in his eyes. Her lips swollen, her face flushed, her brown eyes opened wide with pleasure. The desire in her eyes mirrored his.

"Yes," she murmured huskily. She didn't know what she was doing—and she didn't care. She only knew she ached for the man holding her in his arms, the man whose kisses caused her heart to race and her blood to heat.

He kissed her again with urgent, demanding, possessive lips. She responded eagerly, meeting each kiss with equal fervor, entangling her fingers in his hair and arching her neck as he showered a hot trail of kisses up and down its slender length.

"Why not right here?" she murmured brazenly. "I don't think I can wait until your room."

He grinned at her. Straight, white, beautiful teeth flashed in the darkness.

"What a bold suggestion from a maiden fairy."

She smiled languidly at his teasing. "Who said I was a maiden fairy?"

He chuckled. "I'm glad I came to this party."

Chloe fluttered her eyelashes. "Because of me?"

Max's hot, appreciative stare made Chloe flush. "Most definitely because of you."

She grabbed his tie, glancing over his shoulder and surveying the surroundings. "We're all alone. Make love to me, my super spy."

He moaned and covered her lips with his again. She didn't mind when he pushed her roughly against the uneven bark of the palm tree; the coarseness of the bark seemed to escalate her arousal. She felt reckless, completely and totally reckless, and she thrilled at her inhibition. No one would ever believe she would do something so outlandish, so erotic, and so totally passionate.

He suddenly pulled away.

"What?" she asked. She could hear disappointment in her voice. She didn't want him to stop. She never wanted him to stop.

Concern mingled with desire in his blue eyes. "I don't want to take advantage of you."

"I'm not drunk."

"Really?" He wiggled his eyebrows at her. She noticed for the first time how perfect they were, black and thick, but not Peter Gallagher thick.

Chloe slapped him playfully on the shoulder. "Really. I can drink a few glasses of wine and still be in control." And she wasn't drunk. Okay, so she might be a bit tipsy. But she knew what she wanted, as clear as a California day: she wanted him. She wanted him bad. The ache between her legs throbbed with a fiery intensity.

He gave her a wicked grin. "I want you out of control."

She kissed him hard. "Make me out of control," she challenged.

The passion in his eyes darkened. He held her close, held her tight, and she cried out, rubbing her body hungrily against his. When he sucked at her neck, the edges of his teeth grazing her sensitive skin, Chloe thought she would die from want. She clung to him, her knees weak, her body tingling.

"Max," she moaned softly. "Oh, Max."

She could feel his smile against her skin. He pushed away the bodice of her Regency-style dress. She felt the cool October air upon her skin. And then she felt his tongue, moist and hot, on the swell of her breast. She cried out in pleasure. His mouth closed over her nipple, and she writhed against him.

"Yes, oh, yes," she murmured.

Her hands tangled in his hair. Her heartbeat accelerated. She wrapped one long leg around his waist, pulling him closer with the pressure of her calf until his hands cupped her backside. His fingers inched the silken fabric of her gown up the curve of her leg, and she purred in delicious rapture when she felt the tips of his fingers tease the lace edging of her underwear.

Suddenly, common sense loomed its sensible head.

"Max." It was a breathless sigh.

"Yes, gorgeous?"

His fingers caressed her inner thighs. She trembled and clutched at his broad shoulders. Her insides turned to liquid honey.

"Protection?" she whimpered.

He drew back. His ebony eyes smoldered. "Not with me. Not here."

Her heart plummeted. She couldn't in good conscience make love to a strange man without a condom. She splayed her fingers across his chest.

"I don't have any either. I'm not the type of girl to sleep around. And I didn't expect to meet someone like you at this party."

"Someone you couldn't resist?"

She saw his teeth flash in the shadows. Her heart flip-flopped. Gosh, he was sexy. And she wanted him. Oh, boy, did she want him. At that moment he seemed just as important—if not more so—than the air she breathed.

"Max—"

"Come up to my room."

"But—"

Max pressed hot and urgent lips against hers. She shuddered and returned his kiss. It was deep and thorough and unbelievably erotic.

"Upstairs. I have all we need in my bedroom."

His husky voice tickled her ear. She turned her face to him, and he captured her lips with his again so she couldn't breathe. It was heavenly. He was irresistible, and she didn't even know his last name. Her mother would faint dead away at her behavior.

"Okay," she murmured.

He took her hand and led her across the pool area, through the lobby, and to his seventh-floor room. They almost lost control in the elevator. His searching, passionate, hot kisses drove Chloe out of her mind. She kissed him while he fumbled for his room key, brushed her hands over his pulsating arousal, unbuttoned his shirt, and whispered seductive words into his ear. When at last he swiped the key and pushed open the door, he pushed her into the room roughly, slammed the door behind them with his foot, and crushed her to the wall.

"You drive a man mad." He began to undo the long row of buttons down her back.

She laughed. It was a low, sultry, spicy laugh unfamiliar to her ears.

"Got to get this dress off." He unhooked the last pearl button, and the dress slid forward.

Chloe watched him in fascination. He pulled the dress from her body. It shimmered in the soft light drifting through the window and landed in a pool at her feet. The fairy wings, connected to the dress, glowed in the midst of ruby softness. Her bra soon followed. Max dipped his head and started to suckle her. Her cries were impossible to stop. His fingers wrapped around her wrists, and he pinned her to the wall.

"Max!" she screamed. She felt she would climax simply from his foreplay.

He practically tore her lace underwear from her pulsing body, kissing her bare shoulders and her belly and the gentle swell of her hips.

He swept her up in his arms and carried her to the king-size bed, where he dropped her upon it and then vanished for a moment. She lay sprawled across it, encased only in her thigh-high black stockings, every inch of her skin tingling and alive. Light shone from the bathroom. She saw his reflection in the mirror as he rummaged for the condom.

"Found it." He held the small package up triumphantly, switched off the light, and returned to her side.

"I feel lonely all naked by myself."

"Well, we don't want that." He smiled at her again, that amazing, sexy, adorable smile.

It was Chloe's undoing.

"I need you now, Max. Now."

"And I need you."

She kissed him hard. He shrugged off his tux jacket and white shirt; then he ripped open the package at the same moment Chloe unzipped his pants. He was naked as a jailbird in no time and armored for penetration. Chloe couldn't wait any longer. She wrapped her legs around his waist, and they tumbled onto the bed in a flurry of entwined limbs, scorching kisses, and caressing hands.

Chloe was hot and moist and ready for him. He was hard and throbbing, and she guided him with insistent hands towards her center.

"No more foreplay," she whispered. She gazed into his blazing eyes. "Now."

He plunged deep inside her and she closed around him, welcoming him home. His mouth smothered her scream of ecstasy as his long, driving strokes caused her insides to tremble and pulse. Her body moved in perfect sync with his. She thrust up against him, sheathing him deeper inside her. When her head hit the headboard, she hardly noticed—her body was a river of pleasure. It was pure bliss. It was like touching a bit of heaven. Nothing could compare.

He held her close against him, raising her body to meet his. One of his hands cradled her head, the other her lower back. She climaxed first, and her orgasm sent her sprawling back onto the bed. He came seconds later, collapsing on top of her heaving body.

For a moment, neither said a word. Chloe could hear his rapid breathing and feel the erratic pounding of his heart. She held him gently in her arms, kissing the top of his dark head. He was beautiful—the most beautiful man she had ever been with—and she didn't want to let him go.

"Stay with me." He elbowed his arms on either side of her head.

She glanced over at the clock. Only ten o'clock. She had two hours to spend in the warm cocoon of his strong arms. Looking back into his handsome face, she knew leaving now was not an option—she needed a good cuddle.

"I'll stay."

He kissed her. She kissed him back.

"But I have to leave at midnight."

He pulled out of her body with tantalizing slowness and curled against her, spooning her tenderly. She sank against his strong frame, closed her eyes, and released a happy sigh.

"You are amazing."

His complimentary whisper made her smile. "Thanks."

His lips brushed her collarbone. "I mean AMAZING."

She giggled, making small circles on his forearm with her fingers. "Thanks. And no words can describe you."

"And you thought I was cocky about knowing how to dance," he uttered into the curls of her hair. "Now I'll really be impossible."

A comfortable silence descended around them. It wasn't long before Chloe heard his breathing slow. She called his name softly, but he didn't respond. She turned slowly towards him and found his eyes closed—he was fast asleep.

For the next two hours she watched him sleep. She kissed his nose and his lips and the curve of his cheek. And on the stroke of midnight, she rose from the warm bed and grabbed her discarded wardrobe, which was littered all across the floor. As she slipped into Queen Mab's velvety dress, she spied a magazine on the nightstand beside Max's bed and skimmed her fingers across the glossy cover. Her eyes widened when she spied Max's face. His charismatic smile caused her heart to flutter.

"What the—?" She picked up the magazine and walked to the bathroom, pulling the door halfway closed behind her and flipping on the light. She gasped in surprise when she read the headline: *Romalia's Prince Max Stars in Reality TV Show.*

"Omigod!" The magazine nearly slipped from her fingers. She glanced back at the bed, where Max was still snoring peacefully. Apparently he hadn't heard her startled outburst.

Why didn't I recognize him? He's the most famous prince in the world, and I didn't know who he was?

"I just slept with the world's most famous bachelor!" She clutched the magazine so tightly the pages crumpled. "And he might be my co-worker!"

She was shocked, completely floored. This was not the best way to begin a professional working relationship. Chloe sat down on the toilet and flipped the magazine open to the article. She quickly skimmed it and was relieved to read he denied any truth to the rumor he was slated to star in an upcoming reality show.

Well, he didn't actually deny it. He stated he was not going to comment on the subject. The show's title wasn't listed.

"It's only coincidence," Chloe murmured aloud into the quiet room. "He couldn't possibly be starring in the show I'm hosting. It just isn't possible."

But it could be. She knew that. It *was* too much of a coincidence. She didn't know much about the EVE Network's show due to the fact there was extreme secrecy connected to the project. Even she, the hostess with the mostess, was left in the dark. However, she did know two things: one, it was titled *Courting His Royal Highness*, and two, it was about a famous royal bachelor and his dating escapades.

Chloe suddenly felt very ill. This was definitely not the best way to start on the right foot at her new job. She had never wanted to be one of those girls who slept her way to the top. She refused to be categorized that way.

This can't be happening. He just can't be the prince of my show. No way. Fate wouldn't be so cruel.

But common sense told her he most likely was. After all, she had met him at the party. For what other reason would he be a guest at EVE's annual Halloween bash?

He *had* to be the royal blue-blood who was to star in *Courting His Royal Highness*.

She stood, tossed the magazine onto the counter, turned off the light and opened the door. Then she tiptoed past the bed and exited the room as quickly as she could. She was too mortified by her passionate actions of a few hours before to look back at the sleeping prince.

As she stepped into the elevator and pressed the button for the lobby, she noticed how her fingers shook. In fact, her entire body trembled. And it wasn't a result of passionate lovemaking. She couldn't wait to go home. She'd had enough excitement for one evening.

Sam greeted her at the entrance to the hotel. He tipped his hat to her. "Did you have a good time, Miss Tanner?"

"I did." She ducked quickly into the backseat, hoping he didn't catch the blush highlighting her cheeks.

Chapter Two

She was the sexiest woman he had ever encountered. She gave a new name to desire. He felt as though he would never be able to drink his fill of the mysterious and passionate Chloe, a.k.a. Queen Mab of the Fairies.

Max groaned and rolled over onto his back. The bed seemed immensely lonely without the alluring Chloe sprawled out next to him. He glanced over at the clock—it blinked back at him that the time was 10 a.m. He had a meeting scheduled for noon. But the last thing he wanted to do was talk business. He groaned again and buried his face in Chloe's abandoned pillow. He could still smell her scent, a faint combination of apples and cinnamon.

The fragrance was an instant catalyst to memories of the previous evening. He closed his eyes and breathed deeply as images of long dark hair and black eyes filled his mind and more erotic scenes played like a movie in his head. He saw Chloe writhing excitedly beneath him, her soft, breathless voice urging him to make love to her, her arms wrapped around his neck, her lips hungrily devouring his, her hips rising up to meet his every thrust.

And just like that, he was turned on again.

A knock at the door brought him out of the dreamlike state. Max cursed his aroused condition, grabbed his discarded boxer shorts off the floor, and slipped into one of his favorite T-shirts. It was overly large and hid his erection from sight.

He tried to think of something other than the

sexual, lustful, irresistible Chloe. He would only waste time thinking about her. It had been a one-night stand, nothing more and nothing less. He doubted he would see her again. Good grief! He didn't even know her last name.

Max pulled a shaking hand through his dark hair before peering into the security peephole. His personal assistant stood out in the hallway, looking not at all pleased. Great. Eric Von Stratton. Definitely not the first person Max wanted to see the morning after a night of mind-blowing sex.

He sighed and opened the door.

"What happened to you last night?" Eric Von Stratton plowed past Max into the room.

Max rolled his eyes heavenward. "And a good morning to you, too."

Eric sniffed imperiously. He pushed up his round glasses and flipped out a large black book. "You were supposed to be networking last night. I didn't expect you to vanish after only a couple of hours."

Max ignored his accusing gaze. "Breakfast?" he asked. He closed the door, walked past Eric, and then sat on the bed and picked up the phone. "Well?"

"I've already had breakfast, thank you very much."

"Well, I haven't and I'm hungry." Max quickly put his order in. His stomach grumbled rather loudly at the mention of French toast and scrambled eggs.

"So, where were you?" Eric looked down his nose. "And don't tell me you were with a girl. I've grown tired of that excuse."

Max grinned. Eric had been his closest friend since the age of four. They were as different as night and day, but Max couldn't do without him.

"Then you don't want to hear why I left the party early."

"You attract women like honey attracts bees.

But you refuse to choose one and settle down. No wonder your family is fed up with you."

Max waggled his eyebrows. "I can't help it if I'm attractive."

Eric smoothed his perfectly pressed suit. "You're a cocky bastard. Of course women find you attractive—you're royalty. They all want to be princesses. Every little girl dreams of it."

Max stretched out on the bed. He propped up pillows against the headboard and laced his fingers behind his head. "She was spectacular."

Eric raised an eyebrow. "Oh?" He grabbed a chair and sat down, placing the oversized black appointment book on his knee. "So, tell me about her."

"I don't know much about her except for her name."

"And?"

"Chloe."

"Nice name."

"That's what I said."

"Last name?"

Max shrugged. He stared up at the ceiling.

Eric stared at him incredulously. "You are unbelievable. You must remember who you are. Max, you're not like other men. You must be more cautious."

"What am I supposed to do, Eric? Background checks on every woman I want to sleep with?"

Eric nodded. "That would be a start. She might have been a tabloid reporter. Now the whole world will know what she thinks of you in bed."

"That's ridiculous. Besides, I'd receive only glowing reviews." Max grinned.

"As crazy as it sounds, it could happen. Just look at all the rubbish they print about Prince William."

"I don't need a lecture," Max grumbled. He received enough of that from his mother and siblings. Being a prince was exhausting. It was a full-time job just to remember correct protocol. Most of the time he was in trouble—lots of it—for not following the royalty rulebook.

Eric smiled sympathetically. "I'm sorry, Max."

"Have I told you lately how much I hate being a prince?"

"Yesterday"—Eric glanced at his Rolex watch—"at about this same time."

"Well, I'll say it again and again and again. I'd rather be a regular guy."

"But you aren't a regular guy."

Max sighed in defeat. "Yeah, you're right. I've got duties to perform. I've obligations."

"Like marrying and having heirs."

He grimaced. "That sounds so medieval." He hated feeling like a horse put to stud. "So, what does my family think of our little plan?" he asked.

"They aren't happy."

"Angry I didn't talk about it with them first?"

"Them, and the Romalia Royal Council."

Max was not a big fan of the Romalia Royal Council—the designated ruling body of his country. The fifteen-member council advised the royal family on everything. Heck, the council even picked out the shape of soaps in the guest bathrooms at the palace. Max thought the council too controlling and wanted to dissolve the governing body entirely. But doing was not within his power. At least not yet.

Max preferred to live his own life, which was one of the reasons he loved America. The United States was a nation where a man could be true to himself and pursue and achieve his dreams. It was a refreshing change.

Max didn't really know what his dreams were. He'd never had time to think about what he wanted—his country always came first. He was a prince, and the duties and responsibilities of a prince came before individual dreams and aspirations.

"But they can't do a thing about it."

"Well, you did sign a contract with EVE. They are mad as hornets, but they agreed you must fulfill the contract."

Max grinned. For once he got to choose. It was a thrilling victory.

"They also see a chance to generate some money into Romalia's economy. You'll probably be a big hit. American girls will flock to Romalia just to catch a glimpse of the famous prince. Think of all the money they'll spend."

"So, they win and I win."

"Well, we certainly hope you find the girl of your dreams." Eric pointed at the black appointment book. "Get showered and changed. We have a meeting to get to."

Max yawned. He jumped off the bed and walked into the bathroom.

"Hurry up."

"Why did they schedule a meeting on Saturday morning"—Max squeezed out Crest toothpaste onto his bright red toothbrush—"especially after a big bash like last night's?"

"No idea. I guess they're in a hurry."

"I wonder if I'll ever see her again."

"Who? The girl from last night?"

"Yeah."

"Who cares? You had one hot night. You'll have dozens of women from all over the world to pick from. You'll soon forget all about this Chloe girl."

Max started to brush his teeth, staring hard at his reflection. He doubted it. No man could forget Chloe. And why would he want to? She was gorgeous and sexy and warm and feminine. Most of all, she had somehow managed to weasel her way under his skin—which was not an easy thing to do.

Nope. He wasn't about to forget her. He just

wished he had met her before he started his new job. Starting today, he was off limits for the women of the world—except for the fifteen women who would compete for his affection on the reality TV show he'd agreed to star in. But doing the show was his choice, the first choice he had made on his own in years. And it felt good. Damn good.

****

Chloe was having a bad day. First, her cat vomited all over her new Anne Taylor suit. Then the only two pairs of nylons she owned managed to snag and run. She quickly applied self-tanner, but it turned her skin a horrible shade of orange. She raced to the mall, but Victoria's Secret declined her credit card when she tried to purchase a new pair of hose. She did manage to come up with enough cash to buy the nylons after digging in the black hole that was her purse. To top it off, she spilled hot tea—blueberry-flavored—on her favorite pink blouse.

Staying up late last night and indulging in a forbidden tryst between the sheets was now affecting her day. She possessed not a drop of concentration. She couldn't stop thinking about him: the James Bond dead-ringer with the fabulous eyes and flirtatious smile, muscled biceps and amazing hands. Ah, yes, those wonderful fingers that had touched her most secretive places. Max. Lusty, hunky, handsome Max. Last night she'd experienced pure nirvana—that was truly the only way to describe it.

She needed to stop thinking about Max and start thinking about her job. She desperately wanted to give a good impression to the executives at EVE. Okay, so they had already hired her for the position and she had signed a contract, but Chloe knew from experience things seemingly too good to be true often were. This job could open doors she never knew existed. It was her chance to make it big, and she had no intention of screwing it up. She'd do whatever they asked. She'd be whomever they wanted. She was their puppet. Right now, this job was more important to her than breathing.

"Chloe Tanner to see Mr. Carridine and Ms. Lewis." She flashed the security guard her EVE Network I.D. He returned her smile and waved her in.

"Take the elevator to the sixth floor, Miss Tanner."

"Thanks," she said, smiling as she walked past him through the swinging glass doors into the network's headquarters.

It was an impressive lobby. Skylights decked the ceiling and the walls were made of windows, allowing the California sun to stream in. Palm trees and tropical plants decorated the black-and-white tiled entrance. The centerpiece of the room was a massive waterfall. Chloe felt as though she had just stepped into a tropical forest.

She walked up to the elevators and pressed the UP button. The gold doors, engraved with the network's name, glided open without a sound. She took a deep breath and stepped inside. The doors shut behind her.

Her heart started to race wildly as the elevator zoomed up to the sixth floor. So much was riding on this job. Her career depended on the show being a success. What had ever possessed her to agree to be hostess of a show shrouded in the utmost secrecy and to sign her life away on a legal binding contract? EVE basically owned her for the next two months. And she had no clue what she had signed on for.

For the first time in a long time, Chloe doubted herself. Perhaps it wasn't a good idea to jump into the ocean without checking for nets. They might ask her to eat pig intestine or worse, like those poor fools on NBC's *Fear Factor*. But she didn't think so. *Courting His Royal Highness* had to be something along the lines of FOX's hugely popular *Joe Millionaire* from a few years back, or ABC's *The Bachelor* and *The Bachelorette*. At least that was what she hoped.

The elevator came to a smooth stop, and the doors swept open to the sixth floor.

"Miss Tanner?"

There was no turning back now. The receptionist had seen her.

Chloe forced a smile on her face and strode towards the receptionist. "Yes, I'm Chloe Tanner."

"Mr. Carridine and Ms. Lewis are waiting for you in the conference room."

Panic made Chloe's heart flutter. She looked at her watch, a fashionable pink thing from Target. "I'm not late, am I?"

The girl laughed. "Not at all. They just happen to always be early." She rose from her desk and offered her hand. "I'm Karen. Welcome to EVE."

Chloe shook Karen's perfectly manicured hand. She looked not a day over eighteen, probably a high-school dropout who couldn't wait to make it big in Hollywood. She most likely thought working at EVE was the first big step into stardom. Chloe had once felt the same way. She'd even worked as a tour guide at Paramount Studios and operated the rides at Universal Studios, but not one agent had signaled her out. It was hard to be discovered.

"You can call me Chloe."

Karen's smile was bright and friendly and genuine. "I'm glad to meet EVE's next big star."

Chloe blushed. "Oh, I doubt that, but thanks for saying so."

"Well, these reality television stars are hugely popular. I wouldn't be surprised if you ended up winning an Oscar someday."

Chloe laughed. "Now you really are dreaming."

Karen shrugged one slender shoulder. "It never

hurts to dream. And sometimes dreams turn into reality—especially here in L.A."

Her innocent optimism was refreshing. Chloe hoped Karen's dreams—whatever they were—would come true.

"Yeah, sometimes dreams do come true."

Karen grinned. She was rather pretty, with wide green eyes and flaxen hair. She was also incredibly tall—definitely model material. Chloe guessed she'd find an up-to-date portfolio behind the desk, just in case someone important walked through the elevator doors.

She followed a talkative Karen down the hallway covered with glossy posters of favorite EVE programs and shows, paying little attention to what the cheery young girl said. She could only think about the meeting with Mr. Carridine and Ms. Lewis. She had never been so nervous. Her belly butterflies were now swarms of locusts, and she felt sick to her stomach. She hoped she wouldn't embarrass herself by upchucking all over her new bosses. That would not be a good impression to set the first day of the job.

They paused before Conference Room #1.

"Ready?" Karen asked.

Chloe nodded.

"You'll do fine. Besides, they've already hired you."

"That doesn't mean they can't fire me."

"Don't worry. They aren't going to can you. They like you. I've heard good things."

Chloe wasn't sure how a receptionist knew so much, but Karen's comment softened the nerves pinching her stomach.

"You should be a professional cheerleader," she commented as Karen rapped lightly on the heavy oak door.

Karen flipped a long strand of blonde hair over

one shoulder. "I was."

"I'm not surprised," Chloe chuckled. Yep, Karen was definitely a half-full type of gal.

Mr. Carridine opened the door. He was a tall, stately man in his early 60s, with salt-and-pepper hair and a dazzling smile. He was an important man at EVE Network, second only to Ms. Lewis.

"Chloe, how nice to see you again."

It surprised her when he grabbed her hand and brushed a feathery kiss across her knuckles. She didn't really mind. It was nice to be treated like a lady for once. Some feminists would be outraged by such treatment, but Chloe still appreciated a man who opened the door for her and placed a protective hand on the small of her back.

"I'm looking forward to being part of the EVE team, Mr. Carridine."

He took her elbow in his palm and steered her inside. The door shut softly behind them. The room was simply decorated in soothing tones of blue and green. A long table lined with twelve green leather chairs highlighted the middle of the room, while a comfy couch hugged one wall. A couple of overstuffed matching chairs took up space in one corner.

"I insist that you call me Lester. Being addressed as Mr. Carridine makes me feel so old."

A light, feminine chuckle resonated throughout the room. "You are old, Les."

Chloe turned to face Ms. Antonia Lewis, EVE Network's charismatic CEO. She was a decade younger than Lester and had been in the biz since the age of four, when she'd starred in a popular television commercial. She had worked her way up the ladder, and now she was one of the few women at the top in the business.

Chloe knew all about Toni Lewis. All of tinseltown knew how the silver-haired woman had managed to single-handedly turn EVE into a profit-generating phenomenon. Cable television had never seen anything like it before. The ratings were through the roof. Women programmed EVE into their TiVo, addicted to the emotional dramas, light-hearted comedies, biographies, fashion shows, talk shows, and soap operas that rivaled *General Hospital* and *The Young and the Restless* in popularity. EVE knew its market niche well and kept creating programs women wanted and loved.

"Welcome, Chloe. Take a seat. The rest of the crew should be joining us shortly."

"Nice to see you again, Ms. Lewis." Chloe shook the infamous cable tycoon's hand before taking a seat directly across the table from the elegantly dressed CEO.

"I insist you call me by my first name. Everyone here calls me Toni, and I like it that way."

Chloe couldn't help but return the warm smile. Mr. Carridine and Ms. Lewis seemed so nice that her nervous jitters evaporated. She had only met Antonia for the first time at the Halloween Ball, but she had met Lester briefly before the Halloween gala, when she'd tested for the hostess part on *Courting His Royal Highness*. Both had been brief encounters, hardly giving her a glimpse into his personality at all. Of course, anyone who dressed up as the Scarecrow from *The Wizard of Oz* couldn't be all that bad.

"Did you enjoy our little party last night?" Antonia asked.

Chloe smoothed a loose tendril of hair behind her ear. She sat stiffly in the chair. She still wanted to look her best despite the casual atmosphere.

"It was wonderful. I had a fabulous time."

"You looked simply breathtaking in that fairy gown," Antonia said with a pleased smile. "I think viewers are going to fall head-over-heels in love with you. Even without the costume."

Chloe just hoped the viewing public liked her. Otherwise, her career might be grounded before it even took off.

"We didn't see much of you. Where'd you disappear to?" Lester asked. He took a seat next to Antonia.

Chloe had no idea what to say to that question. She could feel the flush heating her cheeks. She glanced down at her lap, staring intently at her laced fingers. She noticed a few chips in her newly manicured nails.

"Lester, leave her be. She probably hooked up with some guy. It's none of our business," Antonia admonished gently. "You don't need to tell us a thing. We're just happy you enjoyed yourself."

Chloe looked up. "Oh, I did. I had a great time."

"Good."

Receptionist Karen poked her head into the room. "The director and crew are on their way up, and the prince has arrived."

Chloe straightened in her chair. The nervous butterflies returned. Would it be him? She hoped not. But she knew it would be. How many reality TV shows about a bachelor prince could there be? Only one. The very one she was contracted to host.

Antonia smiled at Chloe. "Ah, yes, the prince. Escort him in, Karen."

Karen nodded and disappeared into the hallway.

Lester chuckled. "Chloe, you look so shocked. You knew a prince was involved, didn't you? The title of the show should've been a clue, but you should always be prepared for surprises in reality TV."

Chloe smiled and nodded. She didn't want to give away the real reason for her reaction. What would they do if they found out she had spent a night of pure ecstasy between the sheets with the star of their newest and hottest show? She didn't want to think about it. She decided it was best to play dumb.

"So, we really have an actual prince on the show?"

"Yep. He's royalty through and through. We were thrilled he agreed to do this."

Chloe swallowed the huge lump in her throat. "He's the royal bachelor looking for a bride?"

"Yes. And the fifteen women we chose for this are ecstatic about becoming a princess."

Chloe wouldn't mind being a princess herself. But the idea was so farfetched. Fairy tales didn't really happen. Okay, so she still hoped that somewhere out there was the man of her dreams. But a real Prince Charming? That was a little ridiculous. Even she had to draw the line. Princes did not ride up on white horses, save the day, and whisk the damsel in distress off to their palace for a lifetime of happiness and pleasure. Nope. No way, no how. Living in tinseltown the past ten years had taught her that much. Prince Charming didn't exist, but Prince Scum overpopulated the earth.

"You'll be working very closely with him for the next two months. We hope you'll hit it off."

"Oh, I'm sure we will," Chloe said, forcing a bright smile. Something told her the prince and she would have no trouble getting along. If the man who walked through the door ended up being her James Bond from last night, chemistry would most definitely not be a problem.

There was a knock at the door.

"Come in," Antonia called.

Karen swept in. Her eyes glowed. "Prince Maximilian Alexander Henry Tarleton Radborne of Romalia. And his assistant, Mr. Eric Von Stratton."

Two men trailed behind her. One extraordinarily handsome with his startling blue-blue eyes, an attractive lazy smile, and fine chiseled features. Aristocratic features. She knew the face. She knew it well.

Chloe's heart tumbled to her feet.

It was *him* from last night. Prince Maximilian Alexander Henry Tarleton Radborne of Romalia. Not James Bond. Not a super spy. But a prince. Royalty. Just as the magazine had stated. He was the guy she had to work with for the next two months. She would watch this man—this guy whom she'd spent a very intimate night with—date fifteen beautiful women.

Damn. He looked good, too good in a classy suit with a red tie. But he'd look good in absolutely anything. He'd look just as sexy in an old flannel shirt and faded Levi's. Perhaps more so. He was going to cause American women to swoon. He'd made her swoon, right into his strong arms and into his big king-sized bed.

Chloe wanted to melt away into the floor like the Wicked Witch of the West.

Max spotted her immediately. His blue eyes sparked recognition. His smile widened. His adorable dimple appeared. And he winked at her. He actually winked at her.

Chloe wanted to die.

Her day went from bad to worse in a millisecond.

Chapter Three

Max couldn't believe his eyes. His passionate, exuberant, exotic Queen Mab sat before him.

She looked lovely in a pale pink blouse and black jacket. Her licorice-colored eyes gazed up at him, wide with astonishment, under the attractive sweep of her long lashes. It disappointed him to see her gorgeous mane of hair pulled away from her heart-shaped face in a loose ponytail. A few wisps escaped, softly caressing her flushed cheeks and neck.

What was she doing at EVE? She must work at the prominent network. After all, he had met her at EVE's big gala bash. He felt giddy. Could she possibly be assigned to work on his show? His heart thump-thumped wildly in his chest. He hoped so. Working with her daily for the next few weeks would be a real treat.

"Good to see you again, Your Highness."

Max chuckled at Lester. He shook the older man's hand. "Please don't call me by that horrid title. Call me Max."

Antonia grinned. "Welcome back to America, Max."

Max brushed her outstretched hand with a feather-soft kiss. "You're looking elegant as ever, Antonia."

"Toni."

"Toni."

He looked from his new boss to Chloe. "And who is this beautiful creature?" He thought it best not to give away the fact he knew Chloe. And knew her intimately. He put on his most princely smile and rounded the table.

"We'd like you to meet your show's hostess, Miss Chloe Tanner."

So that's why she was at EVE. She *was* involved with his reality show. Max chuckled inwardly. Fate had a weird sense of humor.

"Ah, Miss Tanner."

Chloe gazed up at him. She looked completely embarrassed and mortified to see him, but he saw just a glimmer of pleasure as well. It was obvious she hadn't forgotten him or the night they'd shared. Who could? It had been one earth-shaking night.

"Your Highness," she whispered breathlessly.

Max grabbed her hand. He noticed it trembled. He recalled how the curves of her nails left crescent-moon creases on the surface of his body. Heat coursed through every inch of him at the memory of her clawing at his back, her voice raspy and filled with need as she embraced him, surrounded him, begged for her climax.

"I insist you call me Max." He swept his lips across her skin. She smelled good. Just as he remembered. Apples and cinnamon. A delectable, delicious, enticing scent. He preferred the fruity fragrance to the expensive colognes sold in boutiques all across Europe. "I've never been one for titles. Always thought them rather pompous."

Chloe smiled at his admission. "Nice to meet you, Max. I'm looking forward to working with you."

He returned her smile. He wished to be alone with her. For a brief moment, he fantasized about taking her in his arms, lifting her onto the conference table, and peeling off articles of clothing ever so slowly. He noticed her short pink and black skirt and the long sweep of her slender legs, legs encased in silky nylon the color of night. Sexy. Damn. He wanted her again. He realized he had never stopped wanting her. She intoxicated him. Drove him mad with desire. He couldn't remember wanting a woman more.

"Well, we have a lot to go over. Take a seat, Max. I'll have Karen bring in information about the show," Antonia said.

It proved difficult to pull his eyes from Chloe. She looked good enough to eat. As he took a seat next to her, his leg brushed against hers, and he noticed the blush on her cheeks deepen at the contact. Her lashes swept against her cheeks as she gave him a sidelong glance. He grinned. She jumped slightly and looked away, focusing her attention on Lester and Antonia.

Karen sashayed into the room, her arms filled with blazing red folders.

"For you, Your Highness."

Max smiled and thanked her, not at all surprised when she blushed and started to giggle nervously. He was used to this reaction. Women were enchanted by princes and usually grew quite tongue-tied around him. He figured it had to do with the fact that little girls were raised with romantic fairy tales. They all dreamed of being a princess and marrying a handsome prince who would shower them with expensive gifts and take them on exotic trips and love them until the end of time.

Damn the Brother's Grimm and Hans Christian Anderson. The real world simply didn't operate that way. It was a nice concept, but it just didn't exist. After all, weren't Princess Diana and Princess Grace evidence of that?

"Max, Lester and I want to tell you again how thrilled we are you agreed to jump on board with this."

Max settled back into his chair, conscious of Chloe sitting so close beside him. His arm brushed hers. Sizzling heat flamed up his arm at the contact.

"I'm looking forward to it," he said.

"Good. Now we have a few things to go over before we send you and Chloe to the location."

"Location?" Chloe asked.

"Yes, we will be filming the show in Arizona."

Max watched Chloe fiddle with the edge of her folder. Her nails were painted pale pink, the color an almost exact match to her blouse. He wondered if pink was her favorite color. He wanted to find out.

"You and Max will be filming in Scottsdale. A good friend of mine agreed to lend her eighty-acre estate for the show. She is honeymooning in Barbados and won't be back until after Christmas."

"We'll be staying there?"

"Yes, you and Max will be permanent residents of the estate for the next few weeks."

Max was pleasantly surprised. The idea of staying with Chloe, tucked away in a secluded estate in Arizona, was very appealing.

Antonia continued, "The fifteen women who have been selected to participate in *Courting His Royal Highness* are already in Scottsdale, awaiting the arrival of their prince charming. However, they are not at the estate yet. They won't arrive until the beginning of the week."

Oh, yeah, the other women. Max had completely forgotten about them. The whole concept of the show revolved around fifteen women competing to gain his affection. Most guys would give anything to be in his position.

"They come from all over and I, along with Lester, personally selected them for the show. I don't think you'll be disappointed, Max."

Antonia grinned at him, and he grinned back. Her enthusiasm was contagious. She was a beautiful lady with a head for the entertainment business. She was positive the show would be a success with audiences around the world, and Max believed her.

He had no reason not to. She had taken a struggling EVE and revamped it, making it one of the most popular networks in

America. Besides, people were fascinated with royalty. Half would tune in just to get a look at him.

But he didn't mind. He was used to the media scrutiny, to dealing with the intrusive lens of the paparazzi. Next to Prince William of England, he was the most photographed royal in the world.

However, it was not a title he appreciated. He would rather live out of the public eye and in seclusion on some remote island. But he had duties and responsibilities to his family and his country— one being to find a wife. And this show was supposed to help solve that problem. This solution was not of the traditional fashion, but he had grown tired of the pressure. And he had always been the rebel in the family, seldom following the strict rules of royal propriety.

Chloe leaned forward. Max glanced at her. Her dark eyes gazed into his for a millisecond, and his heart skipped a beat. A piece of dark hair slipped across her cheek. She brushed it away with those long, elegant fingers, tucking it behind one ear.

"And what is my role in this? I know I'm hostess, but what does that mean, exactly?"

The fragrance of apples and cinnamon wafted up Max's nose again. Just the scent of her was enough to arouse him. He shifted uncomfortably in his seat.

"My dear, besides looking pretty, you'll present each girl to Max. You'll also help him select which two to eliminate each week." Antonia opened the folder and flipped through several papers. "Well, the first week you will eliminate five."

"I get to help him pick?" Chloe asked as she looked over at Max.

Max grinned crookedly at her. He reached out and grabbed her hand, and her fingers curled against his. Her skin was smooth and warm and soft.

"I have absolute confidence in you."

Her dark eyes were huge and wide. Shock illuminated the dark depths. He remembered looking into those eyes when she had climaxed, when he had climaxed, and his heart thundered wildly in his chest.

"We do as well," laughed Antonia. "We know you will make a great team."

Max lifted Chloe's hand to his lips, feeling her shudder as he kissed the ridges of her knuckles. She looked away and pulled her hand from his. He wished they were alone. Making passionate love to her sounded like a great way to spend a Saturday afternoon.

"Okay, so what happens in the end?" Chloe asked.

"Well, Chloe, it is rather simple. One woman will fulfill the lifelong wish of every little girl: to marry a prince. At the end of the show, Max will propose to the last woman standing and we'll have a spectacular wedding in the spring, which we'll film. We already have a name picked out for that, *Marrying His Royal Highness.*"

Max's heart squeezed tight when he saw the hurt in Chloe's luminous eyes. He reached for her hand again, but she shrank away from him. This was bad. This was really bad. He was in a contract with a television network to choose a woman to be his bride and to actually marry her. He couldn't have a future with Chloe. She was the hostess of the show, not one of the fifteen women he was supposed to select from. But he didn't care about the other women. He only cared about the woman sitting beside him, with glistening tears shining in her brown eyes.

"Chloe, I didn't know you were hostess of this

reality show. They told me they'd selected a lovely woman whom I would meet today. I promise I didn't know," he whispered. He reached for her again. His fingers lightly brushed the back of her hand.

She shook her head and sank further back into the chair, managing a small smile. She looked over at Antonia. "The audience will love it. They'll tune in every week to watch Prince Max and his hopeful princesses-in-waiting."

"I know!" cried out Antonia with overzealous enthusiasm, completely oblivious to what was transpiring between her two stars. "Isn't it fabulous? It will be the biggest event in television history! Don't you agree?"

Max's heart ached as he watched the emotions flit across Chloe's face. He had hurt her. He had hurt her deeply. Yes, they had not made a commitment to each other. But he couldn't convince himself their night of passion meant nothing. It did mean something—he just didn't know what. And he doubted he would get a chance to figure it out, thanks to this ridiculous television show.

For the first time since he'd signed the contract with EVE, Max was filled with regret.

How could he work with Chloe every day for the next six weeks and not hold her and kiss her and be intimate with her? How could he date fifteen other women and think about marrying one of them, when all he could think about was the pretty American girl sitting next to him? She was lovely, with snowy skin and dark hair and even darker eyes. Her smile caused his heart to trip.

He couldn't. But he knew he had to.

What he wanted to do was pursue the strong feelings he had for Chloe. But that was out of the question. He was under contract, and so was she. And they wouldn't get a chance to be alone. For the next six weeks, other women, camera crews, producers, directors, and the hundreds of other people it took to make a television show would surround Chloe and him.

What had he gotten himself into?

Heartbreak. That was what. And a whole lot of it.

****

Her job was to help him find a wife, his princess, and eventually his queen. This seemed above and beyond hostess duty. She was actually going to help him select his bride.

This couldn't be happening. She was physically and emotionally attracted to Mr. Prince Charming. And she had no chance with him. Absolutely zilch. She felt sad, betrayed, and just a little bit angry. The handsome man at her side, the man with whom she had shared a most erotic night, was off limits to her. Completely.

Chloe busied herself with studying the red folder in front of her. The show title's letters were purple, the color of royalty, and a golden bejeweled crown tilted at an angle off the H of Highness. She kept her head lowered, hoping no one would see the tears in her eyes. But Max had seen them. She couldn't hide her feelings from him. She closed her eyes briefly and tried to will the tears away, but they lingered, burning behind her lids, threatening to fall at any moment and embarrass her in front of her new employers.

Why did she feel this way? Why? She barely knew the guy. In fact, she didn't really know him at all. She knew his body. She recalled the heat of his skin against hers, the way his muscular form covered hers, the way he held her close to him with his strong arms. Her heart flip-flopped.

She glanced at him out of the corner of her eye. He flashed a dimpled smile at her, and her pulse fluttered. She looked away. Her friends would never believe this one. Not in a million-zillion years.

Antonia rambled on about demographics and ratings to a room filled with people who would be working on the show, but Chloe wasn't listening at all. Her interest in the show faded in comparison to the interest in the man—correction, prince—who sat beside her in his double-breasted suit. His leg kept brushing against hers under the table and he smelled clean, of soap and shampoo. She gathered her courage to look at him again and was relieved he had turned his attention from her to his assistant, who was loudly and forcefully voicing the concerns of the infamous royal family of Romalia.

She nearly sighed at Max's beauty. He was the most handsome man she had ever seen. Heck, Disney would be smart to design all their fairy tale princes after Prince Maximilian Radborne. His dark hair curled over the tops of his ears and against his temples, reminding her of Patrick Dempsey. She liked it a little long. Images of tangling her fingers through his hair flamed bright in her mind, and heat coursed through her. She felt her cheeks turn pink; in fact, her entire body turned pink.

Egad, but this man did things to her. He made her feel totally out of control—and she didn't know whether to like that or not. It was exhilarating and scary at the same time. She knew nothing about him, except that he was an expert in the bedroom. She couldn't remember a time when she'd been so turned on, her orgasm so shattering. Their intimate night together had proved Prince Max was no stranger to women. He knew what they wanted and knew how to please.

A twinge of jealousy gripped her, and she was surprised by it. After all, she had nothing to be jealous about. She had no claim to Max. They had promised no commitments to each other. It had been one utterly amazing, incredible, fulfilling night—and that was all that would ever exist between them.

Sadness replaced the jealousy.

What if Max was the man of her dreams, the man of her heart, and she couldn't have him?

It was too horrible to contemplate.

"Chloe?"

She jolted out of her thoughts at Antonia's voice. She looked up and found the entire room gazing at her.

"Are you all right, dear?"

"Um, yes, I'm fine," Chloe said softly, trying hard not to look at Max. "I'm sorry. I guess I zoned out for a minute. It won't happen again."

Antonia's smile was kind. "Even I have a tendency to daydream now and then. We all do."

"I don't blame you for tuning us out. Once Eric starts talking, it can get boring." Max chuckled. "You don't need to concern yourself one bit about my overprotective family. They're bent out of shape about the whole show. I sort of did this on my own without telling them or getting approval. They aren't very happy with me at the moment."

"Max, they have every right to be concerned," Eric scolded from across the table. "They only have your best interests at heart, as do I. You have an image to uphold."

Max rolled his eyes heavenward. Chloe swallowed a giggle. She could tell by their interaction the two were more than merely advisor and prince. They were friends.

"Mr. Von Stratton, I promise we will discuss the royal family's concerns at a later time in a more private setting,"

Antonia said. "Perhaps we could meet at the beginning of next week. I would be more than happy to talk with you."

Eric snapped his expensive briefcase shut. "I look forward to the meeting. I have a long list."

Max rolled his eyes towards the ceiling again. Chloe and Eric were the only two who noticed. Eric glared at Max while Chloe fought back a spontaneous giggle. He was sexy and funny, a marvelous combination. He didn't fit into the classic stereotype of a stuffy, arrogant monarch. Instead, he was relaxed and jovial, with his lazy smile and sparkling blue-blue eyes.

"I'll have Karen arrange something immediately. She knows more about my schedule than I do." Antonia laughed. "Honestly, I don't know what I'd do without that girl."

"Karen's a gem," agreed Lester. He gathered his papers, organizing them into one neat pile. "There is just one more thing to tell Chloe and Max."

Max leaned forward at the same time she did. Her arm touched his, and she could feel the ripple of his muscles beneath the designer suit. His magnetic blue eyes looked into hers.

"I hope you two don't have any plans for this weekend."

"Well, I was looking forward to relaxing by the pool," Max said with a lopsided grin.

He was adorable. Handsome. Charming. Charismatic. What woman in her right mind could resist him? Chloe knew she couldn't. Spending the next few weeks in seclusion with him at an eighty-acre estate in ritzy Scottsdale was going to send her hormones into overdrive. Big time.

"Your pool lounging will have to wait."

"And why is that, Lester?"

"Well, Max, you and Chloe are booked first-class on a flight to Phoenix tonight."

She couldn't believe her ears. What? She was heading to Phoenix today, and with the Prince of Romalia as her companion? She wasn't opposed to traveling, but she definitely wasn't ready for this. She felt the heat of Max's gaze, but refused to look in his direction.

"Is there a problem, Chloe?"

"No problem. I'm just surprised," she whispered softly.

She wasn't about to complain. This show promised to be her big break into the business, but she couldn't help but be a little irritated. After all, it would've been nice to have some time to pack and make arrangements for her cat. It had never occurred to her she would be leaving so soon. In fact, it had never occurred to her that she would leave California. She supposed she should've been prepared for the possibility. But she was new to this whole thing. And she had a feeling the surprises were just beginning.

"This should be interesting," Max chuckled as he reached for the electronic ticket Lester handed him.

Chloe grabbed her own. "Why is that?"

He shrugged, tucking the ticket into the inside pocket of his jacket. "I've never flown commercial."

She stared at him in disbelief. "Never?"

"Nope."

"Miss Tanner, the prince has his own private jet," explained Eric, "which is undergoing some repairs at the moment."

Chloe narrowed her eyes at the annoying man. He was treating her like a five-year-old, and she didn't appreciate it.

"It'll be fun, Eric."

Eric shook his head. "I must object to this. He cannot travel this way. The repairs on Romalia One will be completed in a couple of days. They can go then."

Riding in a private jet sounded too good to be true to Chloe. So did first-class. She had never flown first-class before. Heck, she barely could afford a coach seat. The last time she'd traveled, really gone on vacation, was at the age of sixteen, when her entire family splurged and went to Walt Disney World. That had been a magical trip. She still remembered her first glimpse of Cinderella Castle. It still filled her with awe. She wondered if Max lived in a castle like that.

Max held up a hand to ward off Eric's objections. "Eric, you can fly out to Arizona on the jet when the repairs are fixed."

Eric opened his mouth, but Max stopped him before another word escaped.

"No, Eric," he said firmly. "The conversation is over."

Eric crossed his arms over his chest and glared at his employer. "Your family wouldn't approve. I don't approve."

Max sighed. "Let's not go there, Eric. Drop it, okay?"

Chloe sympathized with Max. Sometimes she wished her family participated more in her life. She missed them dreadfully and had thought about moving back to Minnesota many times; however, she enjoyed her freedom, her independence, and the ability to make decisions for herself. It sounded as if Max didn't get to make his own decisions and had to have the constant approval from his advisor-friend Eric and his blue-blood family. Jeez, that sucked.

Chloe made a mental note to call home before she left for Arizona to thank her parents for having enough confidence in her to let her be an adult, regardless of how many foolish mistakes she made. And she had made plenty, but she had learned a whole lot in the last ten years. And she'd learned it all on her own. It had not been an easy road, but it had been hers and hers alone.

"A limo will be waiting for you Sky Harbor Internatioanl. It'll take you to my friend's estate and will be at your beck and call throughout your stay."

Max winked at Chloe. "Sounds like fun."

It did sound like fun. It sounded like a romantic getaway for two people in love. But that wasn't the case. They weren't in love. And they didn't have a chance of falling in love, of being together, because she was not one of the fifteen beautiful women who would soon do battle for his affections.

Chloe swallowed nervously. A feeling of impending doom washed over her. She had feelings for Max. She couldn't deny it. One didn't share an extraordinary night with a man and simply not experience some emotional upheaval.

But she couldn't act on those feelings. To do so would jeopardize her career and burn some serious bridges in Hollywood. Making Antonia and Lester angry would be the death of her dreams of a successful acting career. She couldn't afford to do that.

She wasn't sure how this would work. She was going to be alone with him for two days. Oh, heavens, no! Just looking at him made her heart somersault and her palms sweat.

Somehow she found her voice. "When do we leave?"

"The flight leaves L.A. at six tonight. I've instructed the driver to take you and Max to one of my favorite restaurants for dinner. You'll simply love it," Antonia said with a bright smile. "You'll have one night alone together before the contestants arrive tomorrow night. I hope you'll become good friends."

Chloe thought Antonia looked rather pleased with herself. Sort of like the cat who stole the milk. She wondered if there was something she didn't know about this reality show. But it was more likely Antonia was thrilled the show was finally going to start production. Chloe decided not to dwell on it or become paranoid. She had a tendency to do that. She needed to stop worrying so much and let herself enjoy things as they came instead of psychoanalyzing everything. Not everyone had an agenda. And Antonia only had good intentions; after all, she wanted the show to succeed.

The doors to the boardroom flew open and in walked a slew of waitresses and waiters, dressed in pristine white, with trays and serving carts laden down with delicious luncheon goodies.

"Lunch is on EVE today." Antonia beamed. "We want to thank you all in advance for the fabulous show you're going to create. Lester and I know it'll be a smash hit, definitely the type of show everyone will be talking about around the water coolers at work. It will revive the popularity of reality television."

Chloe couldn't believe her eyes. She had never seen so much food. Scrumptious smells filled the room, and her stomach rumbled. She'd forgotten to eat breakfast. She'd been so worried about the meeting.

"Would you and Max do the honors of cutting the cake?" asked Antonia.

A waiter handed Max a silver knife just as a gigantic sheet cake appeared, carried by four waiters. The cake was white, but the letters spelling out the show's name were a brilliant royal purple.

A champagne glass materialized in Chloe's hand. She was so astonished by all the grandeur, she nearly fainted. Her fingers trembled on the elegant stem. It was not made of cheap plastic—it was actually real glass or crystal. She couldn't tell which, but it was definitely not one of the dollar cups she bought on New Year's Eve for the lame party she and Julia hosted every year.

Max smiled at her. She couldn't help but smile back.

"Shall we?" he asked, nodding his head towards the massive cake. It practically covered the entire table.

She couldn't speak. She nodded and rested her hand over his. His skin was warm, and the pads of her fingers slid softly in the valleys between his knuckles.

"To Prince Max and Miss Chloe," toasted Lester, "who will make *Courting His Royal Highness* the most popular reality show in history."

A chorus of cheers erupted around the conference room. Everyone raised glasses in the air. Chloe didn't have time to be nervous, although it did seem like a lot of pressure to put on two people.

Max lowered the knife. Chloe's forefinger covered his as the blade sank into the butter-cream frosting.

She shivered as Max leaned close. His breath tickled her neck.

"Are you ready for an adventure, my Queen Mab?" he whispered.

Her eyes locked with his. "I'm ready," she whispered back.

His lips were so close. She'd only have to move a few inches to kiss him—and she wanted to. She had wanted to kiss him since the moment he walked into the room.

Max's glass clinked against hers. "To us," he murmured.

"To us," she repeated, mesmerized by the deep blue of his eyes.

Her heart trembled.

Realization dawned on her.

She was falling for him. Hard. So very hard.

Chapter Four

The incredulous look on Julia Montgomery's face was almost comical.

"I can't believe it!"

Chloe winced. The cat was out of the bag: she had let everything slip to her best friend and roommate. Julia knew about the show, about her starring role, and that it involved one of the most sought-after hunks in the world, the Prince of Romalia.

"I can't believe it!"

"You already said that." Chloe pointed out the obvious as she threw open her closet doors. She reached in and blindly pulled out an armful of clothing.

Julia flung herself across Chloe's bed. "Wow. I just can't believe it."

"You're starting to sound like a broken record."

"But it's so amazing." Julia sighed.

Chloe tossed the clothes on the bed. "I shouldn't have told you. Nobody is supposed to know. You have to promise me you won't tell a soul."

Julia nodded. "I promise."

Chloe didn't believe her. She loved her friend, but Julia couldn't keep a secret. It was her only fault. Chloe sat down on the bed and grabbed Julia's hands. "I mean it, Jules. You can't tell anyone. My career may depend on it."

"I cross my heart," vowed Julia.

"Why don't I believe you? Why do I think the moment my back is turned, you'll call up everyone we know and blab to them about my new job and the prince?"

Julia's blue eyes grew huge. Chloe had always envied Julia's eyes—but then, she envied many things about Julia. Jules was gorgeous. Blonde. Leggy. Perfect. She looked fabulous in a two-piece swimsuit. She fit the stereotype of a California girl. Except she wasn't from California. She was from Wisconsin. A Badger fan, a Packer fan, and a lover of cheese—all kinds.

"I'm a vault," Julia promised. "I won't say a word. I promise. I know how much this means to you."

Chloe gazed into her friend's eyes for a long time. Though she saw honesty and determination shining in the very blue depths, her heart sank. She knew her friend too well. She could only hope that for once Julia would understand the importance of the situation and not spill the beans.

"Thanks, Jules."

"I'd do anything for you. You know that, don't you?"

Chloe impulsively hugged her. "I know. It's just that this job is so important to me. It's EVE's top secret, and no one is supposed to know about it, at least not yet. If word gets out—"

"I promise, Chloe. I'll make you proud. I won't tell anyone your secret."

"I'd appreciate it," whispered Chloe as she hugged Julia tighter. She was hopeful, but she doubted Julia would keep her word. Julia was a loveable and loyal friend, but a blabbermouth all the same.

"Chloe, it's going to be so hard not to tell anyone," Julia whined softly. "This is big stuff. I mean HUGE. You're going to be a star. It's so exciting. And you get to spend time alone with the world's yummiest bachelor."

Chloe glanced at the clock on her nightstand.

She groaned. There wasn't much time—the limo was picking her up in ten minutes. She untangled herself from Julia and jumped off the bed.

"You'll watch Domino?"

Julia hauled the purring black and white cat into her lap, gently scratching the feline behind the ears. "Of course. You know I love this old thing." The cat's purring increased in speed and volume, appreciative of her affectionate fingers.

Chloe paused a moment to drop a kiss on the cat's pink nose. She would miss her 16-year-old pet. She'd adopted him from a pet shelter her first week in California because of overwhelming loneliness. He'd been her loyal companion ever since. Domino slept with her every night, curled up in a purring, contented mass near her head.

Julia leaned back on the multitude of pillows stacked up against the headboard, which was actually an old antique door she and Chloe had found one weekend at a flea market. They loved shopping flea markets and spent many hours searching for unique treasures. "So, tell me about him."

"I don't have time." Chloe flipped up the bed skirt and fumbled blindly under the bed for her suitcases. She crowed in triumph as she pulled forth the first navy blue piece.

"Come on. You can't tell me this news and then leave without filling me in on all the delicious details."

Chloe struggled to find a second piece to her matched set. She stretched out on her belly and shoved her arm as far as it would go into the lint-filled mystery world under her bed. "Gotcha," she exclaimed as her fingers curled around the handle.

"Come on. Details. I want details. I'm your best friend; therefore, I'm entitled to know everything."

"Who says?" Chloe asked. She stood up and

brushed off her jeans, lint and dust and who-knows-what fluttering off and drifting soundlessly to the floor. "Gross. We really have to clean more around this place."

"It's a rule."

"I've never heard of that rule."

"It isn't written down."

Chloe placed her hands on her hips and raised an eyebrow. "Oh?"

"It's an unspoken rule that exists between best friends."

Chloe wasn't about to tell Julia the rest of the story: that Prince Maximilian was the man at the Roosevelt Hotel. That bit of news would put Julia into overdrive. She'd really demand details. And Chloe wasn't prepared to give them to her. First, she wanted to hide her feelings about Max for as long as possible. It wouldn't take long for Julia to figure out he'd won her heart. Second, there was something so incredibly sacred about that night. Sure, the sex had been fantastic—but it was more than that. So much more. And Chloe couldn't even begin to explain what that was.

"Spill. Now."

Chloe tossed up her hands. "There's nothing to tell. Can't this wait? I'll have so much more to tell you when I get back."

Julia blanched. "But that's almost two months away. I can't possibly wait that long."

"He's fabulous. Hot. Sexy. Charming. Perfectly adorable," she finally confessed. She walked over to her dresser, another old battered flea market find with rusted knobs and peeling blue paint, and pulled out a handful of colored Victoria's Secret panties. "Are you satisfied now?"

"Hardly," Julia snorted. "I think there's something you're not telling me."

"I'm not lying to you, Jules."

"Okay, maybe not lying, but you're keeping something from me. That's not fair."

Chloe flipped open one of the suitcases. "I promise to tell you everything and anything when I get back." She tossed in the underwear and walked across the room to grab matching bras—she hated wearing underwear and bras that didn't match. "But I don't have time now."

Julia snapped her fingers. "I know what you're not telling me."

Chloe threw the tangle of bras in with the panties. She paused in her packing to stare at her friend. "What?"

"You aren't the hostess. You're one of the girls he gets to choose from," Julia said excitedly, as if she had just solved some great mystery.

"Way to go, Nancy Drew," Chloe muttered sarcastically.

"Damn. Not true?"

She slammed her suitcase shut, zipped it, and secured it with the miniature lock. Then she tied a bright green ribbon around the handle. "Nope. Sorry. I don't get a chance at becoming the next Queen of Romalia."

"That blows."

Chloe smiled. "I'd rather be the hostess. Royalty is for the birds. I don't think this guy can pick out a tube of toothpaste on his own. He's got to have approval for everything." She stuck out her tongue in disgust. "Not the type of life for you or me."

Julia gaped at her. "You've got to be kidding. I'd kill to be a princess. It'd be so cool. All that money and fame and—"

"The grass is always greener on the other side," Chloe interrupted as she quickly folded a few skirts and shirts, stuffing them into the second suitcase. She grabbed a few pairs of shoes from the floor of her closet.

"Ah, come off it, Chloe. I know you better than you think. You'd love to be a princess, too. Every woman would. That's why we're so fascinated with royalty. We all want to be Cinderella."

"Yeah, look where it got Princess Diana."

"Okay, that's an exception."

"Princess Grace."

Julia stuck out her tongue. "You're morbid."

"Being royal does not guarantee happiness."

"But it does guarantee a few things."

Chloe groaned at Julia's dreamy sigh. "Enough. I'm not going to be a princess, and neither are you. We'll be lucky if we can pay next month's rent."

Julia grinned. "I'm relying on you. I shouldn't have to work after this gig of yours. We'll be set. You'll be famous, and I'll be your assistant."

Chloe reached into the closet and grabbed the carry-on that matched her luggage set. "Don't you want more than that?" Chloe asked as she ducked into the bathroom to pack a few necessities. Julia dreamed of being a model. Her idol was the ageless American beauty Christie Brinkley.

"Don't forget protection," Julia called.

Chloe stuck out her head and glared at Julia. "Very funny," she said, ducking back into the tiny bathroom the two of them shared. It connected their bedrooms.

"Well, you never know. Imagine getting laid by a prince."

Chloe walked out of the bathroom and shook a hairbrush at her best friend. "Believe me, I'm not getting anything for the next few weeks. I'm going to work my ass off, and hopefully I'll get noticed and be hired by a soap opera or sitcom or something."

"What about movies?"

"I'm not aiming that high yet. One step at a time," she said, tossing the hairbrush into her luggage. "I have to get through this first."

Julia grabbed her hand. "You won't forget about little old me, will you?"

"What are you talking about?"

"When you make it big—and I know you will—you won't forget me, find a new BFF?"

"Of course not. How can you think such a thing?"

Julia shrugged. It broke Chloe's heart to see the tears shimmering in her blue eyes. She pulled her into a suffocating hug and kissed the top of her loyal friend's head.

"You're my best friend. I'll never ever forget you. Remember, we're going to live in a huge mansion someday and have fabulous parties and drink champagne and eat the most expensive chocolate we can find and have endless walk-in closets."

Julia giggled. "Sounds great."

It did sound great. They had fantasized about it since the day they met eight years ago at an audition for a shampoo commercial. Neither got the job, but it'd been the start of an incredible friendship.

"And I'm relying on you to slap me silly if I ever get too big-headed for my britches." Chloe pulled away and checked the time again. Yikes. Her time was up. The limo was probably waiting for her on the street outside their apartment. She bolted off the bed. "I've gotta go, Jules. I'll call you as soon as I can."

Julia grabbed one of the overstuffed suitcases. "You need to learn how to pack." She moaned as she lifted the navy piece and carried it out the door. "Ever heard of less is more?"

"I hardly had time to pack as perfectly as you do."

Julia's grin stretched from ear to ear. "I'm going to miss you. How am I ever going to survive without you?"

Chloe patted her shoulder. "I'm not going away

forever, silly girl." She slipped her carry-on over one shoulder and hoisted the largest suitcase with a grunt. "Ugh. This is horrible. I really need to get better luggage, the type with wheels."

Julia was struggling to carry her piece of luggage down the stairs. "Is there anything breakable in here?"

"Nope."

"Good." She glanced over the railing. "No one below." She gave it a hard shove.

"Julia!" cried out Chloe as the bag catapulted down the stairs to the floor below.

"Well, you said nothing was breakable," Julia called over her shoulder.

"I still don't appreciate my luggage being thrown like that," Chloe mumbled.

By the time she reached the first floor, she wished she'd tossed her bag down the stairs too. Her arms ached. Her back was killing her. Her hands throbbed. She had packed too much. But she was going to be gone for almost two months. How did a person pack for that? Her longest vacation had been ten days to Disney World. And after those ten days, she couldn't wait to get home to her own room, away from her annoying siblings and grumpy parents. Okay, she'd loved the Magic Kingdom and the castle, but family vacations were overrated. Really.

"There's a limo out front," squealed Julia. "You are soooo incredibly lucky."

Chloe dropped the heavy luggage. "Ask me if I'm lucky in six weeks, okay?"

Julia looked away from the front window. "Okay. I'll ask you then. Promise me you'll tell me everything."

"I promise, Jules."

"One more thing."

"Yes?"

"Would you sleep with him if you had the

chance?"

I already have. But she couldn't say that to Julia. Not yet. Later. Much later. When this crazy ordeal was finally over.

But there was no need to lie.

"Oh, yes," Chloe said softly, remembering the simmering night at the Roosevelt. "If I got the chance."

"He's that handsome?"

"To die for."

"Better than in photos? On TV?"

Chloe nodded.

"Wow."

"Yeah, wow," agreed Chloe, wondering again how on earth she was going to keep her hands off Prince Charming for the next few weeks. She'd already sampled the goods, the best she'd ever had. How could she possibly return them, him, now?

Julia glanced out the window again. "Is he out there?"

Chloe shook her head. "I don't think so. I'm sure he has his own private limo to pick him up. Antonia and Lester never said anything about us sharing a ride to the airport."

"I think he's here," Julia whispered.

Chloe's eyes rounded. "What?"

"He's here. At least I think that's him walking up the sidewalk."

"No way."

Julia looked over her shoulder, her eyes wide. "Way," she repeated softly.

It couldn't be. No. He wasn't picking her up. They weren't sharing a limo. No. This couldn't be happening. No way.

Chloe hurried to the window. She pulled back the curtain, noticing her hands trembled. She looked out into the California sunshine and gasped.

Way.

Prince Maximilian strode up her sidewalk, looking deliciously handsome in washed-out jeans and a white T-shirt. Not at all like a prince, but like a regular American guy.

"That's him, isn't it? I mean, I've seen lots of photos of him and read lots of articles about him, but I've never really seen him."

"Yes, that's him."

"Wow. Hot."

The corners of Chloe's mouth turned up at Julia's amazed voice. "Think he's sexier is person? I don't have much to compare to, considering you're the one obsessed with magazines focused on celebrities and royalty."

Julia rolled her eyes. "Ah, you aren't totally oblivious to *People* magazine. You just aren't as infatuated as I am."

"True." Although Chloe did occasionally read the latest gossip about actors and actresses, she had never really been interested in European royalty. She knew about the family Windsor, but that was about it. It was Julia who was enthralled by their comings and goings and romantic interludes.

"How are you going to keep from jumping his bones?"

"I don't know. I just don't know," Chloe admitted softly. "I've been wondering that all day long."

"I take it back."

"What?"

"You being lucky. You might just be the unluckiest woman I know—or at least the most sexually frustrated."

"Gee, thanks."

"I mean, you're going to be tortured every day, watching him date other women, kiss other women, select another woman to be his bride." Julia shivered. "Horrible, absolutely horrible. Can't you switch roles with someone?"

Chloe wished she could. Boy, did she ever.

What a fine kettle of fish she'd gotten herself into. What a fine kettle of fish indeed.

****

The door flew open before Max could ring the doorbell.

He grinned. Chloe stood in front of him, her dark hair floating down about her slender shoulders, her chocolate-brown eyes gazing up at him in surprise.

"Hi."

"Hi."

She looked good, deliciously good, dressed in low-rise jeans and a silky camisole of pale green. The scent of apples and cinnamon drifted about him, embracing him.

"I hope you don't mind."

"What?"

"I suggested to Toni and Lester that we could ride to the airport together."

Chloe leaned against the doorframe. She peered over his shoulder at the sleek black limo. "Yours?"

He glanced over his shoulder and then back at her. "Yep. Guilty."

She smiled. "A private plane. Your very own limo. What's it like to be you?"

He shrugged. "It has its perks."

"I bet," she laughed.

He loved her laughter. She had a beautiful laugh—loud and real and unpretentious. It was a refreshing change from other women he knew. Most were snobs and tended to think laughter and a sense of humor were not attractive feminine qualities.

Max was definitely looking forward to spending some time alone with Miss Chloe Tanner. He wanted to hear more of her laughter and watch the emotions flicker across her expressive face. Her chocolate eyes sparkled. He recalled how they had darkened with passion.

Would he ever forget the night they'd shared?
Probably not. She had already lingered in his mind
longer than any other woman had. There was
something special about Chloe. She affected him.
And very few women could affect him.

He inclined his head towards the two large navy
suitcases at her feet. "Can I help?"

"That would be great. Thanks."

He reached for the piece of luggage and noticed
for the first time the girl standing at Chloe's right
shoulder. Her brilliant blue eyes, as wide as an
owl's, gazed into his. He groaned inwardly. He knew
the look. It was the star-struck look women always
seemed to get when they were around him. He was
used to it, but he still didn't like it. They looked at
him as if he were a god to worship instead of just a
man.

"And you are?" he asked politely, offering the
tongue-tied woman his famous dimpled smile. It was
automatic. It was the smile he used at all social
functions, at royal ceremonies, at charity
fundraisers, and for magazine covers.

Chloe looked mortified. "I'm sorry. I didn't mean
to be rude. Max, this is Julia. Julia, this is Prince
Maximilian of Romalia." She blushed. "I'm sorry, but
I don't remember your entire name."

"It's a mouthful," he agreed. "Even I forget. I
prefer Max. A pleasure to meet you, Julia."

"Prince Maximilian Alexander Henry Tarleton
Radborne of Romalia," Julia sighed dreamily.

Yep, she was completely star-struck. Any
woman who actually knew his complete name was
head over heels infatuated with him. There was no
saving her now. Her eyes glazed over, and her mouth
curved open in an astonished O.

"You actually know his complete name?" Chloe
asked. When Julia didn't answer, still staring in awe

at Max, she turned to Max and apologized. "I'm really sorry. I had no idea she would act this way."

Max chuckled.

Chloe elbowed her astonished friend. "Knock it off, Jules. He's just a guy."

Max gaped at her in pleased surprise. No one had ever referred to him as "just a guy." That was all he'd ever wanted to be—just an average guy who could fall in love with an average gal and have a normal, average life. But that was impossible. He knew that. He would always be a prince; therefore, his life would never be normal. He'd searched the world over for a woman who loved him as a man and not as a prince. But he had failed.

He had failed until now. And now it was too late.

Chloe elbowed Julia again, rolling her eyes when she received no response. "I guess I'll have to apologize for my friend."

"No need."

"Used to it?"

He nodded. "Very."

Chloe leaned close and whispered, "Is this how they always react to you?"

He could hardly concentrate. Her cinnamon and apple fragrance sent his senses into a tailspin. "You mean women?"

"Yes."

"Yeah."

Chloe wrinkled her nose and pulled back. "How awful for you."

"Well, I wouldn't exactly put it that way. It's not such a bad thing having that effect on women."

One eyebrow jutted upwards. "Oh?"

He smiled sheepishly. "I'd be lying if I said it wasn't flattering."

The other eyebrow arched delicately. "I guess so." She gave a low whistle. "Wow."

"Wow what?"

"I just can't imagine."

"I've been putting up with it for years. All part of the job."

"Amazing." She shook her head, and her glossy hair fluttered about her shoulders. Max fought the temptation to reach out and entwine his fingers in the flowing mass. He remembered the soft texture, the feel of the coffee tresses fanned across his chest, the caress of the curls against his face.

"You better get used to it."

"Why is that?"

"Because you're going to be famous, Chloe. This show is going to turn you into a star."

Chloe glanced back at Julia. Her friend still stood in flabbergasted silence. She shook her head and snapped her fingers in front of Julia's eyes. There was no response, no indication Julia even noticed her. Chloe turned back to Max. "Let's hope not."

Max glanced at his watch. "We should go."

"Agreed." Chloe reached behind her and pulled out another suitcase.

"Let me." Max grabbed the suitcase from her. His fingers brushed against the back of her hand, and heat charged through him at the contact. His eyes caught hers, held her gaze. He didn't move. Neither did she. They simply stared into each other's eyes, their hands touching.

"Thanks, but I can manage," she finally said, her voice barely an octave above a whisper. "Really. I can carry it."

He could tell it was heavy, too heavy for her. Why did women always insist on taking their entire closet with them when they traveled? Of course, he owned many pieces of luggage because his station in life required him to dress appropriately. However, he had an entire entourage of employees to organize and pack for him and deliver the luggage wherever it needed to be. Personally, he preferred one duffel bag. It was the only way to travel.

"It's no trouble."

She jutted her chin out and tugged the bag from under his grasp. Her fingers slid from his, and Max immediately missed the feeling of her skin against his.

"I can manage. Don't you know about American girls, Prince Max?"

He took a step back and watched her struggle with the suitcases. "I have a feeling you're about to enlighten me on the matter."

"Ever heard of women's lib?"

"Of course. I'm a firm believer in equality."

"Good." She tried lifting the pieces of luggage and failed. They slammed back down to the ground. "We American girls like to do things ourselves."

Max smothered a grin. "Oh?"

"Yeah. Betcha your European girls aren't like that."

The corners of his mouth curled up. "Betcha?"

She glared at him.

He thought she was the most adorable thing he'd ever seen.

"Are you making fun?"

"Absolutely not. It's just I've never heard anyone use that word before."

"It's common in Minnesota."

"That's where you're from?"

She nodded. "Great state if you can survive the winters."

"I love the cold."

Chloe looked at him as if he belonged in the psychiatric ward. "You're crazy. I'd take warm weather over winter any day. However, I do miss the fall. All those gorgeous tree colors. Does it get cold in Romalia?"

"Yes. Are you sure I can't help you with that?"

He waved towards Roger, his chauffeur. "Roger would be more than happy to help you, seeing as you won't let me. It's sort of his job."

"Nope." Chloe turned around and hugged Julia. "I'll miss you, Jules. Be good. And don't forget to feed Domino."

Julia simply nodded. She hadn't taken her eyes off of Max.

Max swept her a bow. "Once again, a pleasure to meet you."

"Oh, my goodness. Oh, my goodness." Giggles erupted from Julia as he kissed her hand. Her cheeks flushed pink. Her lashes fluttered. She started to fan herself with her other hand.

"Until we meet again, Miss Julia."

Chloe placed a quick kiss on Julia's cheek and gave Max a gentle shove. "Way to go. You're only encouraging it."

"What?" he asked innocently as he followed her down the curving sidewalk. He couldn't resist blowing a kiss over his shoulder at Julia.

Julia squealed and jumped up and down, waving excitedly.

"I saw that. You're incorrigible."

Max couldn't take it anymore. She could barely lift the suitcases, even with two hands. He strode past her and snatched them up.

"Hey."

"I'm all for equality, but I'm also an old-fashioned type of guy, and I like to help out a lady in distress."

"I'm not a lady in distress," she called after him.

He could hear the smile in her voice but didn't look back. All women appreciated a gentleman. He tossed both suitcases into the trunk and slammed it shut.

"Now you aren't going to argue about having the door opened for you, are you?" he asked.

She was smiling. Those velvety eyes sparkled. She tossed a chunk of thick hair over her shoulder. "No. I kind of like having doors opened for me."

"And suitcases carried for you."

She tilted her head and rested her hands on her hips. "Yeah, that too."

Roger tipped his hat to her and opened the passenger door.

Max waved her in. "After you."

She ducked inside.

He followed, but not before blowing one more kiss in Julia's direction. She still stood in the doorway, waving and smiling and jumping up and down.

Chloe poked her head out. "I saw that."

He winked. "Guilty."

"Julia will never be the same."

"Women are never the same after experiencing my charms," he said, sinking beside her on the leather upholstery. He knew for certain he would never be the same after meeting Chloe.

She wrinkled her nose. "Anyone ever tell you that you're rather arrogant?"

He shrugged. "Goes with the job."

"You honestly think you're irresistible?"

The limo moved forward. Max smiled over at Chloe. He didn't see the need to lie. Women liked him. They happened to like him a lot. He'd be a hypocrite to say otherwise.

"Well, I've never been short of admirers. Women have been swooning at my feet since I was a teenager."

She studied him for a moment with her chocolate eyes. "I believe it."

"How about you, Chloe? Have I rocked your world?"

A blush tinged her cheeks. "No," she whispered before looking out the window.

Max knew Chloe Tanner had changed his world, rocked it, tipped it completely off its axis.

And he liked it. He liked it a lot.

Chapter Five

Riding in a limousine stocked full with the very best champagne was quite an experience for Chloe, but flying first-class was overwhelming. The seats were roomy, with tons of leg space. They even boarded first. Chloe had never in her lifetime boarded a plane first. She was usually way in the back, close to the bathrooms—definitely the cheap seats.

"I suppose you're used to this luxury," she commented as Max tucked her carry-on in the overhead bin. She plunked down on the cushioned seat and sighed happily. This was going to be a good flight.

"I'll be honest and say I am. It would be hypocritical to say anything else."

His crooked grin made butterflies flutter in her belly. Gosh, he was dreamy to look at.

Chloe decided it was about time to start paying attention to royal families—especially Max's.

Max shoved his bag into the bin and slammed the door shut before taking the seat beside her. "I'm assuming you're not used to this."

Chloe shook her head. "Absolutely not. Coach was the only way my family flew. And we seldom did that."

"Not big travelers."

She shrugged and fastened her seatbelt. "Never had money to do much traveling. Dad and Mom could hardly leave the farm."

"What type of farmers?"

"Dairy. We also had crops. Can't survive on cows

alone."

He laughed, and his blue eyes twinkled merrily. Chloe loved the way the corners creased. He had laugh lines. She adored laugh lines.

She smiled at him. "Do you think that's funny?"

"I'm trying to imagine you working on a farm. For some reason, the vision escapes me."

She joined in his laughter. "Well, I wasn't very good at it. I did everything I could to get out of chores." She glanced out the window. A sudden wave of homesickness washed over her. Sometimes she missed her family, her home, the slower pace of life, and the security.

"I did the same."

"You?" she asked incredulously, looking at him with wide eyes. "What type of chores did a prince have?"

"Hard to believe?"

"Yes."

"I didn't have to milk cows or work in the fields."

"It wasn't so bad," Chloe admitted.

"Miss it?"

"Yeah, sometimes. Like right now." She pointed an accusing finger at him. "Don't think you can get out of this. I want to know what chores you had to do."

"My parents were firm believers in teaching us responsibility. They didn't want us to become spoiled. We worked in various parts of the palace, but mostly we—"

"Palace?"

He chuckled at her surprise. "That's where we live."

She blushed. "It seems so unbelievable. You must have a fairytale life."

"Most think it," he said softly, "but it is far from that."

She studied him for a moment, remembering his

conversations with Eric Von Stratton at EVE and during the drive to the airport, when Mr. Von Stratton had called and tried unsuccessfully to convince Max to wait for Romalia One.

"I believe you. I'd hate to have my life dictated by a set of rules and people. Maybe you should fire Mr. Von Stratton."

He chortled at that. "He's more than my personal assistant—he's my best friend. We grew up together, and his father is my father's advisor. I trust him with everything—and I don't trust too many people. However, he's always very annoying when we're in America. I like it here. He doesn't."

A file of people marched by, heading to the coach seats Chloe normally occupied. She enjoyed their envious glances as they strolled by. She planned on milking this for it was worth—she didn't know when she'd fly first-class again. A glass of white wine was a definite must.

"So, name some of the chores you had to do."

"You're persistent, aren't you?"

"Very. I once considered a career in journalism."

"What made you change your mind?"

She made a face. "Do you know what a journalist makes?"

"Not really."

"Well, we're talking just above the poverty line."

"That bad, huh?"

"Yeah. Of course, I'm pretty much there right now. So, did you make beds or mop floors or something?"

Max leaned back in his seat and stretched his legs. "I did."

She was awestruck. A prince with millions and servants at his beck-and-call, who actually got dirty doing housework—it was unheard of. "At the palace?"

He shook his head. "Charity work. We

volunteered." A dark curl curved over his eyebrow. He brushed it away with a sweep of his hand, his fingers snagging through his midnight hair. "Although I wouldn't call charity work a chore. I enjoyed it, and so did my sisters and brother. We enjoyed being out with the common people."

Chloe burst into laughter.

"What's so funny?" His startled blue gaze made her laugh even harder.

"You."

"Me?"

"Yes. The common people? Is that really what you call us?"

The sky-blue of his eyes darkened to sapphire. "Not you."

Her heart danced. Her breath quickened. "Not me?" she whispered softly.

He covered her hand with his. "You're far from common, Chloe."

She trembled beneath his touch. The tender strength of his hand felt incredibly good. The pads of his fingers caressed her sensitive skin. She looked down, watching as he made intricate and seductive little circles on the back of her hand.

"I am common," she murmured.

He leaned towards her, curling his fingers around hers. "Not to me. Not to anyone who has the honor of knowing you."

His husky voice sent shivers throughout her body. She dragged her gaze up to his face, where she was soon lost in the mesmerizing pools of his eyes.

"I'm quite jealous."

"Of what?"

He leaned closer until his nose touched hers. "Of the world."

"Why?"

"Because soon the whole world will know you and be in love with you. You're going to be famous."

Her cheeks flamed pink. "Oh, I doubt it."

"There's something special about you." His gaze swept her face. "You glow."

It was probably the best compliment she'd ever received. Her heart swelled, and warmth spilled through her. She wanted the flight to last forever. And was saddened to know it wouldn't.

"Chloe, don't you think we should talk about what happened between us?"

She didn't think she was ready to discuss it. What was there to talk about? They had no future. He was a world-famous monarch, and she was a farmer's daughter. Nope. No future there.

"I was thinking we should just forget about it, Max." She slipped her fingers from his and clasped her hands in her lap. "I had an amazing time. But now it's over."

"No, I don't believe that. It isn't over. I don't want it to be over. I can't forget about that night, Chloe. I can't get it from my mind. You changed my world."

Another wonderful compliment. She glowed. Now she'd changed his world. She was flattered, more than flattered. It wasn't every day a girl like her heard those words uttered from the lips of a prince.

"Max, nothing can come of it. You're going to choose a wife out of fifteen beautiful women from all over the world." She smiled sadly. "And I'm not one of those women. You can't be with me."

He frowned. "Who says?"

"Have you forgotten about the contract we signed with EVE?"

"For a moment I did." He sighed. "I'm regretting my decision to do this. Maybe Eric and my entire family are right. It's probably my craziest idea yet."

"Why did you do it?" she asked gently. "You can't tell me you have a problem finding dates. I'm sure hundreds of women would jump at the chance to marry you."

Sadness shadowed his eyes, sadness and longing. Her heart flip-flopped. Waves of tenderness crashed through her. She grabbed his hand with both of hers.

"I gave up on finding love. Real love. Not the storybook stuff, but real, passionate, all-consuming love. I wanted to be loved for me—not for my money, or because I'm a prince."

"You couldn't find it."

"I couldn't find it," he repeated. "And so I gave up. I need to find a wife who will be my princess and, eventually, the future queen of my country. I'm thirty-five and not getting any younger. My country needs an heir, and I can't search any longer. Time has run out."

"I can't imagine the pressure. It must be overwhelming."

He lifted her hands to his lips, brushing each finger softly, tenderly. "It is, Chloe. Overwhelming. I made this decision on a whim because I was so tired of not living up to expectations, of always being a disappointment, of being told what to do. I thought it was a good idea at the time. I would pacify my family, my royal advisers, and my people by finding a beautiful wife to make my princess. And I'd also bring some money into the Romalia treasury by increasing interest in my country. It's expected that tourists to Romalia will double after the show hits the airwaves."

A smile curved her lips. "But it sort of backfired."

He smiled back. "When I met you. I never planned on you."

She confessed, "I didn't plan on you either."

"Now what do we do?"

She lifted one shoulder. "I'm not sure. We can't

do anything at all."

"Not now," he agreed.

"Not ever."

"Nothing is written is stone. There are always loopholes."

"Max, I can't risk angering Antonia and Lester. They could blackball me. I might never work again if I jeopardize their precious show. And they aren't the only ones who have high stakes in this show. They've already sold all the advertising."

He traced the curve of her jaw with the tip of his finger. "But there is something here, Chloe. There is something between us. I want to explore it. I want to see where it leads."

There was no use lying or pretending as though nothing had happened, as if that night hadn't mattered one little bit to her. Because it had. It had mattered so very much.

"I'm not going to argue with you. I feel the same. It drives me crazy to think about being so close to you the next few weeks and—-"

"And not being able to touch and kiss and experience a night like we did at the Roosevelt," he finished for her.

"Yes," she whispered. "But we have to try to forget that night."

"Impossible," he whispered back.

His finger brushed across her lips as the plane taxied onto the runway. The flight attendant rambled through her spiel about oxygen masks and floating cushion devices and what to do in a crash landing situation, although Chloe paid little attention. She was crash-landing already—but it had nothing whatsoever to do with the plane.

"Max, I'm serious."

"So am I."

His crooked grin was adorable. Her pulse quickened. Her heart raced.

The plane ascended rapidly into the air as Max's lips descended upon hers.

Chloe knew the smart thing to do would be to stop him. But she couldn't. She just couldn't stop him. She liked being close to him, loved the way his lips snaked over hers, thrilled at the passionate heat bubbling between them. She cupped his face in her hands and melted against him.

Okay, so maybe she couldn't have him for a lifetime, or even for the next few weeks. But she had him all to herself at the moment, and she wasn't going to deny herself the pleasure of kissing Prince Maximilian of Romalia.

But Chloe knew she couldn't let it go any further than a kiss. They couldn't pursue anything more. To do so would only get them into trouble—or at least get her into trouble. Her big break had finally happened, and she wouldn't do anything to jeopardize her dream of becoming a star. It was all she had ever wanted.

But as the kiss deepened and the fire inside her burned brighter, she began to wonder if that was truly all she wanted. There was more to life than an acting career. There was love. She had given up on it. And then Max, her James Bond look-alike, her authentic Prince Charming, had waltzed into her life and made her reevaluate everything.

And made her believe she still had a chance of finding love.

Chloe forgot about the plane. She forgot about first-class travel. She completely forgot about the television show that might launch her into the national limelight.

She could only think of Max and his lips caressing hers.

"Max," she murmured.

"Don't talk. Just feel."

She drew him closer and deepened the kiss. It

felt so good, so deliciously wonderful, that she didn't ever want to let him go. She felt safe and cherished and loved. The palm of his hand slithered down her back; the intricate massaging of his fingers sent red-hot desire rocketing through her.

She felt the plane reach its cruising altitude, leveling out in the clear blue sky high above California. Her ears popped. Her heart hammered. Endorphins spiraled throughout her trembling body. She curled against him, wanting to be closer, needing to be closer, wishing the armrest didn't stand as a barrier between them, longing to be alone with him.

But they weren't alone. Far from it.

"Excuse me."

Chloe heard the voice. She chose to ignore it. She didn't want the embrace to end.

"Excuse me."

Overwhelming disappointment filled Chloe as Max pulled away. He smiled at her, gently, tenderly, his blue eyes almost black with passion. Smokey. Sexy. Her heart danced erratically. She dragged her fingers against his lips, and he kissed each finger. Her body screamed in response to the evocative pressure of his lips.

"I'm sorry to interrupt."

Max turned to the flight attendant. Chloe watched in awe as the practiced royal smile appeared, the smile so many women went weak in the knees over. No wonder it was plastered on the cover of countless magazines across the country and the world. It was a breathtaking smile. Picture perfect. Dazzling. It showcased his straight white teeth and the dimples in his cheeks.

"I was just wondering if you needed anything. A drink, perhaps?" asked the attendant.

Max beamed. A tinge of jealousy pinched Chloe. She didn't want to share him with anyone, especially an attractive flight attendant with a flirtatious smile and vivacious curves. She was definitely dressed in a uniform two sizes too small, leaving little to the imagination.

"As a matter of fact, I would like something." Max looked over at Chloe. "How about you?"

Chloe straightened in her seat and pasted on a smile. "I would love a white wine."

She was glad to be sitting down, because Max's smile made her knees weak. And it wasn't his royal smile. It was not for the cameras or reporters or the world. The warm smile he bestowed in her direction was clearly intended only for her.

"A white wine for the lady, please."

The brunette didn't even look in Chloe's direction. "And you, sir?"

"I'd like a beer."

It sounded funny to hear a prince asking for a beer. But Max was full of surprises. It was just another thing Chloe liked about him. The list was getting long. In fact, she couldn't think of anything she *didn't* like about the guy.

"What kind?"

He shrugged. "I don't usually have a beer," he admitted. "Surprise me."

The attendant laughed and playfully tapped his shoulder.

Chloe winced. It was a fake laugh, a coquettish laugh, the type of laugh only women could see through. To men it was cute. To women it was sickening. The attendant's nametag read "Linda." Chloe didn't appreciate Linda touching her prince.

My prince? Since when did he become my prince?

"I'd also like a pillow and a blanket."

"You aren't considering sleeping?" Max asked. "We'll be there in an hour."

"Nope. I just want to get cozy," Chloe said with a suggestive smile. She slipped her arm through his and pulled him towards her, ignoring the amused twinkle in his blue eyes. "Thanks, Linda. That'll be all."

Linda didn't bother to look Chloe's way. She was staring at Max. "Do I know you?"

"I don't think so," Max replied.

Chloe watched in fascination as realization dawned in Linda's eyes.

"I do know you!" She pointed at him, her fingers shaking with excitement. "You're Prince Maximilian!"

Max's shoulders sagged slightly. Chloe's heart went out to him. She slipped her hand over his and gave a soft squeeze.

"Yes, that's me."

"Omigod! I can't believe it. A prince is on my plane. This is so exciting." Linda's eyes were as wide as saucers. Her hands fluttered dramatically over her heart. "I'm a huge, HUGE fan."

"It's a pleasure, Linda. I'd really appreciate it if you'd keep this quiet. I don't want the entire plane to know I'm on board."

Linda glanced around. She leaned forward with one hand cupped at the corner of her mouth and whispered conspiratorially, "Of course. I completely understand, the paparazzi and all."

Max nodded and continued to smile warmly. Chloe wanted to box Linda's rather large ears. At least she had one cosmetic flaw. Chloe didn't have the patience he did. He was incredibly patient—but then he dealt with this all the time.

"So you understand our need for discretion?"

"Certainly. I won't tell any of the passengers. I promise."

"Excellent. Thank you, Linda."

"You're most welcome, Your Highness."

Chloe giggled at the woman's quick curtsy. Max's look of warning quieted her instantly.

"I'll be back pronto with your drinks." She shot Chloe a deadly look. "And a blanket and pillow."

"Don't think she likes me much," Chloe commented as she watched Linda walk down the aisle. "She sure likes you, though."

"I just hope she keeps her word."

"I wouldn't hold your breath on that one. Looks like she's already filling in her co-workers."

Max glanced up and groaned. Linda was busily whispering something to two other flight attendants. The group of women kept looking back in his direction, smiling and waving.

"I guess Eric was right after all," Max sighed. He snagged a hand through his hair. "I should've waited for my plane. That way we could've avoided this. Sometimes I forget how recognizable I am."

"You do have a face that is hard to forget."

He flashed that smile meant just for her, the one with the dimples. The corners of his eyes crinkled, enhancing the laugh lines she found so attractive. "I do, do I?"

She flushed. "You do."

He lifted her hand and kissed it. "When I was a child, I often dreamed of what it would be like to be an average person living an average life."

Chloe wrinkled her nose. "You don't want that life. Trust me."

"And you want mine?"

"You want to be average. I want to be extraordinary."

His gaze was intense. "You are extraordinary."

"In an average sort of way, I suppose."

"No, in a wonderful, unique, fabulous sort of way."

Chloe's fingers tightened around his. "Thanks."

"Fame isn't all champagne and roses."

Chloe nodded. "I understand that. I just always wanted more out of life, and I thought the answer was to become an actress."

"Fame and fortune can't buy you happiness, Chloe."

"Yeah, I know. It's just I've always been driven. I've always been searching for something. I'm not really sure what it is, but I just know I have to fill that empty space inside me to be happy. I suppose that sounds crazy."

"Not at all. We're all searching. Even I'm searching."

"What are you searching for?" she asked. She was interested to know what a man like Max could be looking for. After all, he had everything. He was hunky-gorgeous, insanely rich, and he was a prince who could have anything he wanted at the snap of his fingers. What more could the guy want?

"I don't know. I just know I'm not complete. Sort of like how you feel."

She wondered if the rest of the world saw the heavy-hearted side shimmering in his sky-blue eyes. She doubted it. People saw him as they wished: the handsome playboy and charismatic prince who lived one of the most glamorous lives in the world.

"Yeah, sort of like me," she whispered.

"Guess we're two peas in a pod."

The corner of her mouth lifted in a trembling half-smile. "Yeah, I guess we are. I never thought I'd have anything in common with a prince."

"Well, now you do."

"Yes, I guess I do."

Linda returned. She tossed the blanket and pillow at Chloe, all the while smiling and batting her lashes at Max. She looked like a teenager with a crush. Chloe ignored Linda's high-school flirting routine, stuffing the pillow behind her head and tucking the blue blanket around her legs.

"Here's your beer, Your Highness."

Chloe rolled her eyes.

"Thank you, Linda. You can call me Max." Max took a sip of his drink. "Delicious choice."

Linda giggled girlishly. "I just knew you'd like it."

Okay, enough was enough. Chloe was beginning to feel ill. "My wine?" she asked sweetly.

"Here." Linda shoved the small bottle and glass into Chloe's hand.

Chloe unscrewed the cap and poured the liquid into the glass. She cupped the glass in the palm of one hand, reclined back in her seat, and took a sip.

"Will there be anything else? Anything else at all?"

"Nothing else."

"Your Highness...I mean, Max, could I ask a favor?"

Chloe indulged in a second sip of wine and gave Max a sidelong glance. Once again, he pasted on his drop-dead-gorgeous smile.

"What can I do for you, Linda?"

Linda leaned close. "Could I get your autograph? No one is going to believe me. No one will believe me. They'll think I'm making it up, probably because I always say I see stars. Of course, I really think they are, but then they turn out to be just regular people."

The look Max threw at Chloe said it all. What he wouldn't give to be one of those regular people, the kind no one noticed when they flew commercial air or when they dined out in a restaurant.

"I would be happy to give you my autograph."

Linda beamed happily. "I'll be right back." She scurried away.

"I don't know how you do it."

Max downed his beer. "Years of practice."

She shivered. "I don't think I'd ever get used to it."

"Well, once this show hits the airwaves, you

might have to. If it ends up being as big a hit as EVE thinks, you'll be recognized everywhere you go."

Chloe's eyes rounded. "Do you really think so?"

"Definitely."

She couldn't imagine what that level of fame would be like. It seemed so impossible. "I should take notes."

"I'm no expert. I just know what works for me."

Chloe spied Linda jogging back towards them. "You must be doing something right. Your public adores you."

He grinned. "Well, I'd rather have them adore me than hate me. That could easily happen. The public is finicky. They aren't loyal to anyone."

"I beg to differ," Chloe commented. She pointed to the two flight attendants following Linda. "You've got a fan club right here."

Max groaned. "Here we go."

"I guess she couldn't keep a secret."

He glared at her. But she saw the amused twinkle in his eyes just before the horde attacked him, pens and magazines poised. She caught a quick glance at the publication and started to laugh. He was on the cover.

"Be quiet," he grumbled under his breath as he smiled his royal smile and began signing his glossy photo.

It wasn't long before the entire first-class section knew the Prince of Romalia was on board. Soon every woman was asking for an autograph and giving Max her complete attention. Chloe finished her wine and snuggled under the blanket, observing Max's interaction with his adoring public.

He really was amazing. He could no doubt charm the world with that dimpled smile, infectious laugh, his genuine interest in whomever he was talking to, and his unending patience.

And she was going to spend the entire evening

alone with him and the next few weeks working closely beside him. Plus she had already shared one incredible intimate night with him. Damn, was she a lucky girl.

Chapter Six

"Trying to be gentlemanly again, Your Highness?" Chloe teased as Max pulled her carry-on from the overhead compartment and refused to hand it over.

Max secured the strap onto his shoulder before reaching for his own bag. "What on earth do you have in here, Chloe? Your entire closet?"

"A girl should never be without her necessities," she pronounced as she slid past him into the aisle.

"I'm interested in knowing what those necessities are," grumbled Max as he followed her off the plane.

Chloe glanced over her shoulder. "Men simply don't understand how much effort it takes to be beautiful. Do you actually think we roll out of bed looking fabulous?" She batted her eyes at him playfully.

His laughter joined hers as they stepped into the America West terminal at Sky Harbor International Airport. "I would bet my kingdom that you're quite breathtaking when you first wake up."

Chloe tilted her head away so he couldn't see the heat staining her cheeks. No man had ever made her blush so much. It was infuriating. She felt as though she had no control over her emotions. She stopped, looking for a sign directing them to the baggage claim area. Max plowed right into her.

She laughed softly, enjoying the warmth and solid strength of his muscled body against hers. "Hey, watch it!"

"Well, you should've warned me you were about

to stop," he whispered into her ear.

The gentle caress of his warm breath caused her toes to curl in her open-toed sandals. For a brief moment she simply enjoyed being so close to him. His lips were tantalizing close to the curve of her ear. She fought the impulse to turn and entwine her fingers in the dark mass of his hair, bringing him closer for a soul-shattering kiss.

"I think the baggage claim is that way," she murmured. It took all her willpower to pull away from him. Somehow she managed. She wasn't sure how, but she felt herself step away from him, leading him towards the claim area.

It wasn't long before he was walking in step with her.

"I've never been to Phoenix."

"Neither have I," she admitted. She glanced around at the Southwestern décor. "But I've heard good things."

"Me, too. Although I'm told it's still blazing hot until the end of October."

"Guess we have a few weeks before it starts to cool down." She stepped onto the escalator. "I like the heat."

He joined her on the stair. "So you've said. Don't you miss the snow?"

She shook her head. "Not really. Around Christmas I do."

"Not an outdoorsy person?"

Chloe chuckled at the very idea. "Absolutely not. My family loved to ski and snowshoe and go sledding. I was never a big fan."

"Do you ski?"

"I do." She stepped off the escalator onto the lower level.

"But I'm not very good at it. I'm more of a beach girl." She pointed towards the carousel that would soon hold their baggage.

He followed her lead. "Hence moving to California."

"Yeah."

"I'm glad you can ski."

"Why? Are you planning on taking me skiing?"

"I'd love to take you skiing. Let's make plans now. How about skiing in the Alps over the holidays?"

Chloe stopped abruptly, almost causing Max to collide into her again. "You're kidding, right? You mean the Swiss Alps?"

His eyes twinkled at her. "I mean the Swiss Alps." He dropped the carry-on luggage on the ground. "And I'm not joking. My family owns a ski lodge, and we spend New Year's there. I'd love for you to meet them."

Chloe didn't know what to say. She was officially being asked to accompany the world's most sought-after bachelor on a trip. Thousands of women would die ten times over to have a chance like this. But how could she accept such an invitation? It was impossible.

"Haven't you forgotten something?"

He arched an eyebrow. "I don't think so."

Chloe crossed her arms. "Well, won't you be wining and dining your new fiancée? Isn't the whole goal of this television show to find you a bride? That's what we signed on for, isn't it?"

The smile on Max's face vanished. He snaked his long fingers through his dark hair. "I sort of forgot about that."

"You're forgetting about it a lot."

"I should've listened to my family. They were right. This is ridiculous."

"I don't think so. You're tired of playing the bachelor gig *and* playing by their rules. So, you made a decision to sign a contract with a major network to be the headliner star of a reality show that will help you find the perfect bride. It might seem a little drastic, but I understand. I really do."

And she did. He was tired of living a life dictated by everyone else. She could only imagine the amount of control that others had exercised over his life from the time he was born. A crown prince destined to become a king. He wanted what everyone wanted: freedom. He wanted to make his own decisions, make his own path. She couldn't fault him that. Who could? Initially, his family might be a little embarrassed by this reality show, but eventually they'd embrace the publicity. Romalia's tourism industry would grow thanks to the show. It might even face an economic boom thanks to its royal master.

"You're the only person who understands. It's comforting to know I have one person on my side." The corners of his eyes crinkled attractively.

Chloe knew she'd never be able to look at a summer sky again without remembering the intense sapphire color of his eyes. She was absolutely positive she would dream about those eyes and that gorgeous smile for the rest of her life.

"They'll come around. After all, *Courting His Royal Highness* is bound to bring in lots of money for your treasury."

"That's the only reason they've allowed this mockery."

She laughed. "Mockery?"

His crooked grin sent fiery sensations spiraling up and down her body. "My father and mother call it a mockery. My siblings agree, but they think it's a splendid way to get me to finally settle down."

"By finding a wife."

"One can only be a playboy for so long. It ruins the reputation of the royal family eventually. Accepted when under the age of thirty, frowned upon when over thirty-one."

"I'm glad I'm not royalty."

"But you'll be Hollywood royalty."

She grimaced. "Do you suppose that's just as bad?"

He nodded. "Are you prepared?"

"No."

"Maybe you'd rather be a princess than an actress?"

Chloe's heart skipped a beat. "What?"

"Well, I'm just saying the possibility is out there."

She brushed her hand against his. "We've already talked about this, Max. We have no future. We shouldn't even speculate. I'm not one of your fifteen choices. I'm the hostess of your show, not a love interest."

But I want to be. Boy, do I want to be.

"I'm not ruling it out."

She couldn't help but smile. Warmth spooled through her. He was one in a million. Rich. Famous. Sweet. Kind. Romantic. Gosh, why couldn't she have met him before, before they'd made the commitment to the show and signed a binding contract? It was a cruel joke. She couldn't let on how much he meant to her. She couldn't let him know she cared for him; in fact, she was afraid she was beginning to love him, which was a dangerous thing to do. He was off-limits. The sooner she accepted that fact, the better.

"I can pay the fee for breaking the contract."

"I can't."

"I'll pay yours as well."

"Oh, Max," she sighed, "think of what that would do to your family. They would be embarrassed even more if you broke the contract. Think of the bad publicity. Besides, we only shared one extraordinary night. It doesn't mean we have a forever."

"I'm still not going to completely give up on you and me." He took her hand in his. "I always get what

I want."

She shivered at his words. His voice and his intense gaze clearly indicated he was indeed a man who was never refused anything. An almost possessive glow lighted his blue eyes, a steely determination to have what he wanted.

He wants me. He wants me.

The bell chimed, signaling the arrival of the luggage. She turned towards the carousel, withdrawing her hand from his. As she did so, her bare arm bumped his, and goose pimples swept up her arm. She trembled and rubbed her arms with her hands. She liked him immensely, and she wished more than anything that she could pursue a relationship with him.

But that couldn't happen. She needed this job to solidify her career. Emotional involvement with him could jeopardize it. Besides, it wasn't as if he'd declared his love for her and asked her to marry him.

Prince Max was only offering more fabulous nights under the sheets. Not love. Their sexual attraction was not the issue. It was mind-blowing. But it didn't create love or a happily-ever-after marriage. Only love did that. *Love.* A future with him was not a sure thing. This job was. And she had to dedicate herself to it. She had to take care of herself. She wasn't about to consider breaking her contract with EVE.

She needed this job more than she needed a man in her life. This was her time to shine. Sure it'd be grand to be a princess, a queen, but that wasn't a guarantee.

What if they threw caution to the wind and indulged in a torrid affair? What if it ended after only a few weeks or a few months and he left her? What then? She'd be broke, jobless, and without Hollywood connections because her name would be mud. She'd probably lose any chance of ever making it big in the business. She'd be sacrificing her dream, and the thought terrified her.

"Yours?"

She spied the matching pieces and nodded. The luggage was a high-school graduation gift from her mom and dad. "Can't miss them. Both have bright green ribbons on them."

He patted her shoulder. "Genius."

"My mom's trick."

"If I traveled commercial, I'd do the same."

"Don't brag," she teased. "I wish I had my own private jet."

"I'll give you a ride in mine sometime."

"Max, I think we should—"

He held up a hand to halt her words. "I know. I'll drop it." He gave her cheek a quick kiss. "For now."

Her spine tingled at the husky promise in his voice. "We missed the luggage," she whispered, turning her face to his. The tip of his nose touched hers.

"They'll come around again. There's always a second chance."

Chloe knew he wasn't talking about the luggage.

She did the only thing she could do. She kissed him.

****

It had probably been a bad idea to kiss Max. But she had anyway. And it had felt deliciously wonderful. No man had ever affected her the way Max did. He was fast becoming an addiction—an addiction she couldn't afford.

Chloe released a miserable sigh as she tossed her purse onto the bed in her new bedroom, the room that would be hers for the next few weeks while shooting the show. She was thankful she'd be sharing this wing of the house with the camera and production crew and not the beautiful women vying for Max's hand. Max shared the west side of the house as well. That could be trouble.

She glanced around the room. It was a huge, amazing room, larger than her entire apartment. She still found it hard to believe people lived in such extravagance. She slipped off her sandals—they were starting to pinch her feet—and traipsed across the room towards the floor-to-ceiling windows. Not a single curtain adorned the windows, allowing for a magnificent view of the McDowell Mountains, which zigzagged along the north edge of the property. The sun was just beginning to descend on the horizon, and purple and red shadows caressed the peaks and valleys of the mountain terrain.

"Wow." She whistled appreciatively as she took in the view. She could get used to waking up every morning and going to bed every night to this picture-perfect landscape. She'd always heard about how beautiful the Sonoran Desert was; now she knew it to be true.

She turned on her heel and studied the room. It possessed a high vaulted ceiling and a sand-colored tiled floor crisscrossed with area rugs in Navajo style. The walls were painted a pale yellow, except for the wall behind the queen-sized bed, which was painted a deep red. Large clay pots and vases, filled with dried flowers in an array of vibrant colors, decorated the room along with statues of geckos, coyotes, and the famous Native American flute player, the kokopelli. A small fountain tinkled soothingly in one corner.

Chloe felt as though she'd just stepped into a spa. It was an oasis far more extravagant than any place she'd stayed in previously. Traveling with her family involved overnight stays at KOA campgrounds or at the Holiday Inn.

"I wonder if I'll ever have a home this

luxurious?" she mused aloud. She hoped so, although she doubted it. She couldn't see herself living in such fancy surroundings. After all, she was still a country girl at heart. She had simple tastes for the most part—except when it came to her shoes and clothes.

She zipped open one suitcase and tipped it on its side. The contents spilled out onto the bed. She quickly tossed underwear and bras into the top drawer of a purposely-rustic dresser in one corner of the room and flipped on the light to what she thought was the bathroom. Only it wasn't.

"Wow!" she cried with a childish clap of her hands.

She didn't really care at the moment if there was a bathroom connected to the room. What stretched before her took her breath away. A huge walk-in closet loomed in front of her, far bigger than her entire bedroom back home. She stepped into the immense emptiness and started to laugh. The sound echoed off the walls, and still she couldn't stop laughing. It was extraordinary. Every woman dreamed of a walk-in closet like the one she stood in.

"I think I've gone to heaven," she whispered with a shake of her head as she pivoted around in a miniscule circle. "Wait until Jules hears about this. She won't believe it."

Chloe didn't waste any time filling up the closet. She emptied all her suitcases. She hung dresses, blouses and skirts on the hangers, and folded jeans, shorts, and T-shirts in the shelves provided. There were even slots for her shoes. After unpacking, she stood back and surveyed her work. She made a decision that she definitely needed to go shopping for more clothes. Too many empty spots glared back at her. Yep, she needed to shop some Scottsdale boutiques.

The attached bathroom caused her to ooh and ah again. A Jacuzzi tub sank into the floor, looking incredibly inviting. The north windows surrounding the spa tub offered breathtaking views of the McDowell Mountains, and a skylight directly above provided an evening bather a great view of the stars. Live exotic flowers and vines tumbled over the ledge circling the tub. To top it off, the bathroom had double sinks, a mosaic-tiled floor, terry-cloth robes hanging on hooks, and a comfy bench covered with a blue cushion and laden with blue, brown, and red pillows.

Chloe wanted nothing more than to indulge in a tub with warm water and fragrant bubbles. But she couldn't. She glanced at her watch and groaned. She only had fifteen minutes to get ready for her dinner date with Max. She caught her reflection in the long horizontal mirror over the sinks and wrinkled her nose. It would take more than fifteen minutes to make her look ready for an expensive dinner with a drop-dead gorgeous prince.

A prince she desired with every breath in her body.

Off-limits. Completely.

"You aren't going to think about him that way any longer," she scolded her reflection. She shook her finger for emphasis. "Absolutely not. He isn't available. Even without the show, he would be unattainable. So just knock it off."

But how could she tell her heart what to think?

It had never worked in the past. And she was positive it wasn't going to work now. Hearts were ruled by emotion, not logic. Logic said to stay away from Mr. Prince Charming. Emotion said to get closer and closer and closer and....

"I said, knock it off!"

She exited the bathroom and slipped into the closet, where she stripped out of her travel clothes and then squeezed her size-6 body into a silky green strapless dress and her size-8 feet into high-heeled shoes of the same color. A necklace and pair of dangling earrings made out of chunky turquoise completed the look. She raced back to the bathroom, ran a brush through her hair, smoothed the unruly strands with a few drops of water, and applied eyeliner, mascara, and her favorite lipstick.

Five minutes later, she grabbed her purse and walked out into the hallway.

From his spot waiting for her at the bottom of the stairs, he looked up at her and smiled his royal smile. She about melted on the spot. He was delicious. Scrumptious, really. A totally irresistible, tantalizing dessert.

Logic said to run like hell.

Emotion said to stay and enjoy.

Chloe smiled back, placed a trembling hand on the smooth banister, and started her descent down to the first floor. Max met her halfway, his contagious grin lighting up his blue-blue eyes.

"You look amazing," he complimented.

"I betcha you tell all the girls that," she chided. But she was secretly pleased. She wanted to look good for him—that was why she'd chosen her favorite dress. She knew the clingy fabric hugged every curve of her body. And the blue-green color emphasized her dark hair and eyes.

He looked dashing in a pair of neatly pressed gray dress slacks and a button-down blue shirt, tucked in snugly at the waist. He was broad and muscled, and his eyes had never looked so blue.

Those eyes really were startling. No wonder women across the world swooned over him and magazine photographers loved him. Blue eyes. Black hair. Olive skin. Charismatic smile. Model bod. Loads of money. European royalty. Posters of his smiling face probably adorned the wall of every female college student in the fifty states, smack dab next to Prince William Windsor of England.

The electric touch of his hand on her elbow as he gently escorted her out the front doors sent excited chills up and down her body. It was amazing what a simple touch could do. His fingers were warm, the pads kneading softly into her skin. Chloe remembered quite well the feel of his hands on her body. He was an expert with those hands, a talented lover. She refused to ponder how many women he'd practiced on before her. She knew in her heart the number would be crushing.

A limo waited for them in the roundabout driveway of the Mediterranean-style mansion. The driver tipped his hat and opened the door. The heat of the Arizona sun still lingered in the evening, the fragrance of a flower she couldn't identify permeated the air, and she could hear the romantic melody of water splashing from a nearby fountain into a tranquil pool.

"Are you ready to dazzle Phoenix with our charms?" asked Max.

She tilted her head slightly so she could view his face. He seemed to tower above her. So broad. So muscular. So spectacularly handsome. An amused smile tipped the corners of his mouth up. And the corners of his eyes crinkled ever so attractively.

I'm in love. I'm in love. I'm in love.

The knowledge was wonderful and horrifying at the same time.

She smiled up at him. "The question is, are *you* ready?" She wiggled her eyebrows at him, challenging him.

He chuckled. His fingers curled about her elbow. She suddenly wished she'd remembered to exfoliate the rough skin. A little lotion wouldn't have hurt either, but she hoped he wouldn't notice. His European sweeties probably exfoliated all the time; their skin was probably as soft as a baby's bottom. Of course, they didn't shave. At least she had that over them. She'd shaved that very morning and was thankful she had. Rough elbows and knees and heels could be forgiven, but not hairy legs.

"Where are we off to, Simon?" Max asked.

Chloe dipped into the limo, her fingers lingering against Max's. She didn't want to lose the skin-to-skin contact.

The driver grinned. "A popular fondue restaurant."

"Sounds delicious."

"It is. One of the best in Phoenix, sir."

Max slid in beside Chloe, and his fingers curled around hers. "Fondue fan?"

Chloe admitted she'd never had fondue.

"Tonight will be a new experience for the both of us." He brushed her knuckles with a kiss. His blue eyes never left her face.

Delicious shivers shimmied up Chloe's spine.

"Cold?"

"No."

He draped his arm about her and pulled her close. She happily rested her head against his chest, closed her eyes, and resigned herself to enjoying this one night alone with Prince Max. They had one night together before the crew arrived—and before the bombshells vying for his attention showed up with their claws extended.

"I want this night to go on forever," he whispered against her hair.

She snuggled close. "Me, too."

The limo lurched forward, slowly rolling down the winding driveway towards the tall iron gates marking the entrance into the estate. The gates swung inward, and Simon steered the luxurious car out onto a road lined with tall palm trees, with white lights circling the slim trunks.

"Do you think you'll be noticed tonight? Have a hundred autographs to sign?"

"I hope not. I don't want any distractions." He kissed the top of her head. "I want to focus completely on you."

"Sounds marvelous," she murmured. And she wanted the same. She wanted to share him with no one. He was hers and hers alone. At least for tonight. After that, she'd have to share him with a television crew, fifteen bachelorettes, and the world.

And have her heart broken all over again.

Chapter Seven

The fondue restaurant was located in one of the many outdoor shopping plazas Scottsdale was famous for. Towering palm trees lined the entrance to the plaza; hundreds of tiny white lights wrapped about the thick trunks. It was a warm autumn night—even in October, the temperatures still soared in the high 90s—and dozens of people sat on outdoor patios laughing and visiting, cooling down with glasses of chilled wine and other thirst-quenching beverages.

A bubbly blonde hostess welcomed Chloe and Max into the restaurant and soon seated them in a cozy booth for two in back. Chloe was disappointed the place didn't have outside seating, but it was a charming place with small secluded booths and soft candlelight. It was very romantic and amazingly quiet. The gentle sound of classical music floated out through nearly invisible speakers in an overhead sound system.

"Nice place," Max commented as he slid in across from her. He grabbed the wine list and thumbed through it. "Drinks?"

Chloe nodded. She unfolded the linen napkin and placed it on her lap. She noticed her knees were shaking and covered them with her hands. This guy—actually, this prince—did something to her. He totally unbalanced her. And she wasn't used to being out of control. Nope. She was an in-control-of-herself gal.

She looked over at Max. He smiled at her over the top of the wine menu. There was no way he could see her knees shaking, but she had a feeling he knew she was nervous. Of course she was; after all, she was having dinner with royalty. She couldn't resist smiling back. His smile was contagious. Heck, *he* was contagious. Yep. A hunky, delicious, contagious disease no woman in her right mind would want a cure for. Unless, of course, there was no way she could have him.

"A favorite?"

"Chardonnay or Riesling. I think I'd like a Riesling."

"Fabulous choice. I think I'll have the same." He folded the menu and placed it in its designated pewter holder at the far end of the table.

A waitress took their drink order and handed them a dark blue dinner menu. She rambled off the specials, flashed a big-toothed smile, and looked Max up and down appreciatively before walking away.

"She was checking you out."

Max glanced up from the menu. "Oh?"

Chloe laughed. "You don't seem surprised."

He shrugged. "I'm just happy she didn't notice who I am."

"Like the flight attendant?"

A wicked grin split his countenance. "Exactly!"

Still laughing, Chloe flipped open the menu. It wasn't long before her mouth was watering. The choices were scrumptious: Raspberry vinaigrette salad, lime-cilantro salad, bread and cheeses, filet mignon, lobster, and shrimp; and strawberries and cheesecake dipped in chocolate fondue for dessert.

Chloe leaned forward. "I think I'm going to enjoy fondue," she whispered.

Max duplicated her move. His hands closed over hers. The warmth of his fingers against her skin sent delightful shivers throughout her body. She liked his touch. She liked his touch so very much. She couldn't recall a man who'd ever had this much of an effect on her. Why, oh why was he unavailable? Why, oh why couldn't she have met him under different circumstances? But without the show, she'd never have met him. It wasn't as though they traveled in the same social circles. Far from it.

"I think I'd like it better if we were alone back at the mansion."

An erotic thought flashed through her mind. Him. Her. Warm, gooey chocolate dripping on their bodies. The very idea of him licking chocolate from the valley between her breasts sent her heart into a tailspin. She wrenched her fingers from his and sat as far back in the booth as she could, as far away from him as possible. She looked down at her hands and nervously played with the edges of the silky cloth napkin.

"I apologize," he said softly, "but my mind is filled with thoughts of you—and they aren't G-rated."

"I know. Me too," she murmured, gazing up at him through her lashes.

The waitress brought their wine. Chloe grabbed her glass and took a long sip.

"Ready to order?"

Chloe glanced down at the menu. The words blurred. She couldn't think straight. Food was the farthest thing from her mind. She craved *him*. She hungered for *him*. She wanted to devour him with her lips and her tongue and....

"We'll have the Couple's Special."

Chloe didn't even know what was in the special, but she didn't really care.

The waitress nodded, batted her lashes at Max, slid the menus from the table, and wandered off again, but not before looking back at Max over her shoulder.

"I think you've got another fan."

Max sighed. "She's pretty, but I'm not

interested. I only have eyes for you, Chloe. I've only had eyes for you since we met."

"We just met." She looked at her watch. "Have we even known each other for twenty-four hours?"

He chuckled. The corners of his blue eyes crinkled. She loved that. Gosh, how she loved that. And he dimpled. Gosh, she loved that too. Was there anything she didn't like—love—about him? Oh, yeah, he was off-limits. That sucked. She just had to keep reminding herself of that fact. Otherwise her heart would be lost. And she couldn't take that chance.

"All I can think about is loving you."

Her heart flip-flopped. "Loving me?" she squeaked.

"Yeah." He took her hand and brushed his lips against the tender skin of her wrist. "Loving your entire body like I did at the party. Making love to you. You were so wonderful, Chloe. You've intoxicated me."

So that was what he meant. He didn't actually *love* her. He simply loved having sex with her. Two completely different things. Opposite ends of the spectrum, really.

"Max, stop kissing me."

He stopped and pulled away, a hurt expression on his handsome face. Chloe hid her hands under the table and tucked her feet under her seat. The best thing to do was to avoid contact with him— when he touched her, she lost all self-control.

She sighed sadly. "What you must think of me."

He raised an eyebrow. "What? You must know I think you're wonderful."

"In bed!" She spoke the words before she thought and was instantly mortified. She covered her face with one hand and then peeked between her fingers and looked around to make sure no one had heard her outburst. But nobody was there to witness it, because the secluded booth was separated from everyone else's. She looked at Max. He was fighting a smile. Nope. He was trying not to laugh. His eyes sparkled. She almost flung her napkin at him. "This is not funny!"

"It is. Didn't we clear this up?"

"Will we ever?" she asked softly, removing her hand from her face and setting it on the table.

"I don't think any less of you because you slept with me on the first date."

She grimaced. "We weren't even on a date. I didn't know you at all."

"We'll call it a blind date."

Chloe groaned and slouched in her seat. "Great. That's much better. So much for Midwestern values." She shook her pointer finger at him. "Don't laugh. Don't you dare."

He bit his lower lip. "I'm trying to convince you that it hardly matters to me. I know you don't make it a habit to sleep with men, and—"

"Strangers. I don't make it a habit to sleep with strangers."

"So, you do sleep with lots of men?"

She gasped. "I most certainly do not."

He laughed. "I didn't think so."

Honeyed warmth flowed through Chloe at the sound of his masculine laughter. It was rich and timbered, and it wrapped her in a cozy, fuzzy, irresistible blanket. She could listen to him laugh all day long.

"Well, I'm certainly not wife-material for a royal prince. What I did with you"—the heat in her cheeks flamed bright—"was very unladylike."

Max snorted. "Nonsense. You're a lady, Chloe. You're more of a lady than half the blue-bloods in Europe."

The corner of her mouth lifted. "Truly? You don't think less of me?"

"Absolutely not."

"But you'd never think seriously about a woman who—"

"I would."

"Would what?" she whispered. His opinion was very important to her. She wanted him to respect her. She wanted him to look at her and not see a passionate one-night encounter, but a woman he could spend the rest of his life with.

"I would because I am. I'm thinking very seriously about you, Chloe. You have no idea how seriously."

Chloe swallowed another drink of wine. She didn't know what else to do. She didn't know what to say to him; she didn't know how to respond. Why had she brought it up? Why? It didn't matter. They couldn't possibly be together. It just couldn't happen.

"It's nice to know, even though—" Suddenly, she couldn't speak a word. Her throat constricted. She looked away from him, at the shimmering liquid in the wineglass. She could use another glass.

"Chloe, what do you think about me?"

She blinked, startled by his question and stared up into his amazing blue, blue, blue eyes. "Pardon?"

"Me. Tell me what you think about me."

"You're a prince."

He rolled his eyes. "Besides that."

"Well, I like you."

"Like me?"

"Yes." Her voice sounded slightly shaky, and his lopsided grin made her want to jump across the table, throw her arms about his neck, and kiss him.

"Well, that's good to know. But maybe you don't think I'm much of a gentleman."

She studied him for a long moment, admiring the breadth of his shoulders and the broad expanse of his chest. "I said I liked you, didn't I? Why would I like you if I didn't consider you a gentleman?"

"Good point. But a true gentleman wouldn't take advantage of a drunk woman."

Feeling insulted, she stiffened. "I was not drunk. Tipsy, maybe, but not drunk."

His eyes widened. His eyebrows lifted. His dimples deepened. She saw the merriment in his eyes. He was enjoying this exchange—and she was too. More than she'd thought possible.

She hoped the food would never arrive. She wanted to talk and laugh with him all night long. It felt natural; it felt intimate, far more intimate than their sexual encounter of the night of the ball.

"Still, a gentleman does not seduce a woman whom he knows is intoxicated."

"You did not seduce me. I seduced you."

He chuckled. "Perhaps we're both to blame."

She agreed and hoisted the wineglass in the air. "Should we toast on it?"

Max lifted his glass. "To being ungentlemanly and—"

"Unladylike," she finished with a giddy giggle.

"Because I wouldn't trade *our* night for anything."

Chloe looked deep into his eyes as their glasses clanked together. "Neither would I, Max. Neither would I."

And she meant it with her whole heart. No matter what happened in the weeks to come, she'd never ever regret the one night they'd shared together. It was too beautiful to regret. It was too real and glorious and magical. She'd never forget. The memories of that night would have to last her for years to come, because she knew she loved the man who sat before her. It was the type of love that was meant to last forever.

It was the type of love that could never be.

She felt like a gloom-and-doom heroine in a romance novel.

Hot tears filled Chloe's eyes as she finished the last of the Riesling, trying not to look at Max. She didn't want him to see the tears; she didn't want him to see how deeply she cared. What was the use? He was going to marry someone else. She wasn't even a candidate to be his wife. Life was not fair. It wasn't fair at all.

The food arrived, and Chloe was thankful for the distraction. She wiped the edges of her eyes with the corners of the soft napkin while the flirtatious waitress leaned between Max and her and set the fondue oil on the built-in burner.

Chloe had no idea how to get through the night. Actually, she had no idea how to keep her sanity over the next six weeks. She'd go crazy being with Max every day but not really being with him.

She couldn't shake the horrible thought of seeing Max with another woman. Her heart constricted tightly just thinking about him kissing someone else. Envy slashed through her, green envy at each of the women who would vie for his attention and ultimately his lifetime commitment.

Max smiled at her, the corners of his very blue eyes crinkling at the corners. The idea of that gorgeous smile focused on another woman broke her heart.

****

Three hours later she was trying to erase the image of Max's handsome face and toe-curling smile from her mind. But it was no use. She was intoxicated, drunk on not only his smile, but on his laugh and on his voice and on his hot, appreciative stares.

She sighed sadly and sank into the soft bench stationed in front of the bedroom vanity, grabbing a brush and dragging it ruthlessly through her mass of coffee-colored hair. She tried to focus on anything but Max. And she failed—miserably. She chucked the brush across the room in frustration, knowing there would be no sleep for her tonight. Zip. Zilch. Nada.

"You're a pathetic creature," she mumbled to her pathetic reflection. "There are plenty of other guys out there, nice guys just waiting to find someone like you."

Her image in the mirror blinked back at her. She released a miserable groan and turned her back on herself. She didn't want to gaze upon the wretch in the mirror any longer. The tears shimmering in her eyes, the trembling of her lower lip, the total anguished and dejected look on her face made her wish to sink into the tiled floor and die.

"I'm made of stronger stuff than this," she shouted into the empty room. "I can handle this. I've got to handle this. My entire future depends on it."

Chloe glanced at the clock. Both hands covered the number twelve. Cinderella's death toll. Just like the night at the masquerade ball. She might as well have turned into a brilliant orange pumpkin. If she had, she wouldn't be dealing with the Max situation right now or the overwhelming emotions he created inside her. Or maybe she would; after all, she'd most likely still be attracted to him, even in pumpkin form.

She stood up and crossed the room to the glass doors leading out onto the verandah. They stood open, letting in the evening breeze. But it was still warm. She stepped out onto the patio and looked down into the immense backyard of the estate. It was breathtaking at night. Lights highlighted curving walkways, exotic palm trees, desert plants, and the flagstone area surrounding the large pool and hot tub. She didn't feel much like a soak in the hot tub, but the blue-green waters of the pool looked very refreshing on such a hot night.

Sleep still eluded her; she needed all her energy

109

to put on a brave face tomorrow. Taping began when the women arrived tomorrow evening, and from that moment on, the cameras would be rolling almost twenty-four hours a day for the next six weeks. She'd have barely any privacy, certainly none with Max. Tonight might be her only chance to take a dip in the tempting pool without prying eyes.

Her decision made, Chloe stepped from her silky robe and pulled on her favorite pink two-piece swimsuit. She knew she looked great in it, which was why it was her very favorite. Of course, no one was going to see her in it. Max was most likely fast asleep in his room down the hall, and she'd be all by herself in the cooling waters of the pool, which included a gorgeous waterfall tumbling over natural stone.

She heard the sound of the waterfall through the open windows. Refreshing water tumbled over rough rocks into the pool below. She couldn't wait to feel it washing over her face and body. Hopefully, it would wash away the heated memory of being in Max's strong arms.

She slipped from her room and hurried down the tiled hallway with an oversized beach towel slung over one shoulder. Her bare feet were silent against the cool tiles; she was happy she'd decided to not wear any shoes. She didn't want Max to hear her. She needed some time alone—time to think.

But what if he feels for me the way I feel about him?

She pushed the thought aside. She'd already gone over this a million times in her mind. She couldn't risk her career, everything she'd worked for, and her entire future on the hope that Max loved her. He was a playboy. He was one of the world's most famous playboys, if not the most famous. He'd had tons of girlfriends and, according to dozens of magazines, left a trail of broken hearts. Yes, there was no doubt he was attracted to her. Yes, there was no doubt he cared—she saw it in his blue eyes—but did he love her? She didn't know. And if he did reciprocate her love, was it enough to bind him to her forever?

Chloe shook her head, hoping to clear it of her rambled thoughts. But it didn't work. Not even a little. She couldn't stop thinking about him. He haunted her. He'd always haunt her.

"Stop it," she instructed as she walked through the foyer and into the back courtyard, where the pool glimmered welcomingly underneath a sky laden with sparkling stars and a moon so huge and large and low, it looked as though she could reach up and touch it.

Chloe took a few deep breaths, focusing her nervous energy on a yoga breathing exercise to calm her rattled nerves. She missed yoga. It'd been months since she'd attended practice, and she definitely needed to get back into the routine. She felt so much better, physically and emotionally, when she did. But she'd been too busy pursuing her career to make time for anything other than job hunting for the past few months. Julia called it an obsession. She was right, but Chloe was determined to hit it big in Hollywood before she turned thirty, and she was already twenty-five. That didn't leave her too much time to achieve her dream.

She'd already decided that if she didn't get her big break before the age of thirty, she was packing up her bags and moving back home, where she'd probably work at the local Wal-Mart for the rest of her life. Lots of Chloe's high-school friends worked at Wal-Mart and were perfectly happy, but Chloe wanted more. She'd always wanted more, and she knew she was meant for great things. She knew it with every fiber of her being.

It wasn't long before her heart rate slowed and

she began to calm down. The silence of the night, broken only by the occasional howl of a coyote and the peaceful splash of the waterfall, soothed her. She took one last breath before dropping the towel on a nearby chair and jumping into the deep end of the pool, where the water encased her in a safe cocoon from Max and the world.

When she at last broke the surface with a contented sigh, ready for an hour or two of peaceful serenity, she nearly plummeted back under to the bottom at the sound of Max's voice.

"I see I'm not the only one who couldn't sleep."

Chapter Eight

Hearing the unmistakable rumble of his all-too-sexy voice shocked Chloe so much, she gulped in a mouthful of chlorinated water. She instantly pushed her way to the surface again and spewed water from her mouth, sputtering a few very unladylike words as she did so. Then she pushed hair from her eyes and glared at Max, who happened to be laughing rather loudly and grinning from ear to ear; his dimples had never looked so darling.

"What are you doing here?" she asked, frantically trying to smooth the matted mass of hair away from her face and hoping she didn't have discharge from her nose smeared all over. Ugh. How attractive was that! She touched her face, skimming her fingertips under her nose. She was clean.

"Can't I enjoy a swim as well?" he asked.

"Of course you can. You just surprised me."

"Obviously. I apologize. I think I almost killed you. Are you going to survive?"

A teasing lilt echoed in his foreign accent. She loved his accent. There had to be something about him she didn't like. No one was perfect. Of course, love was blind. But he sounded perfect and, damn it, he looked perfect: a chiseled example of male perfection. The mold must've been broken after he was made.

Chloe couldn't take her eyes of his bare chest. Droplets of water clung to dark, curly hair; a glowing sheen of water covered his muscular shoulders and arms. His black hair, wet and incredibly sexy, was slicked back from his face. And his heavenly blue eyes watched her intently from under long sooty lashes. He was irresistible. A wildfire of desire swept through Chloe's body. Even the coolness of the water around her couldn't extinguish its fiery heat.

"Chloe?"

She dragged her gaze from his chest to look up into his eyes. Her heart tripped and picked up speed. "I'm fine."

"Glad to hear it," he said, moving towards her. "Although I wouldn't have minded saving your life by using mouth-to-mouth resuscitation."

He was moving closer. She backed away. This wasn't good at all. She couldn't be this close to him without losing control.

And she didn't want to lose control again because it only caused her heartache. It was just her luck that she'd fall helplessly in love with a one-night stand. Why couldn't she be like normal people? Lots of her girlfriends let loose and gave into temptation and didn't lose their hearts. Why did she have to lose hers to Prince Max of Romalia?

"Don't come any closer." She practically shouted the words at him. He paused, clearly startled by the force and volume of her voice. "Please, Max, don't. I can't take this any more. I just can't do it. It's too...well, it's just too heartbreaking."

He gazed at her over the aqua water, which now covered his chest and shoulders. His chin touched the surface.

"You understand, don't you?" she implored softly.

"I understand." His eyes gazed deeply into hers. She felt as though he looked directly into her heart and saw all the raw emotion there. She felt vulnerable—and she didn't like it at all.

"But shouldn't we enjoy each other?" he continued. "After tonight we won't be alone any more."

"Stop it. Can't you see this is torture?"

"For you?"

"Yes, for me," she snapped irritably. She turned from him and swam over to the waterfall; once there, she turned around to face him and wished she could blink him away, just like Jeannie did in the 1960s sitcom *I Dream of Jeannie*. "Isn't it for you?"

"It will be after tonight, when I can't do anything about my feelings," he said, respectfully keeping his distance. "But tonight we can do something about the feelings we have."

What was wrong with men, with Max? Was it so easy for him to have sex with one woman and then move on to the next conquest without any emotional attachment? Chloe couldn't. She'd never been able to be intimate with someone and then nonchalantly say goodbye and move on with her life. She'd been with more than a few jerks in her rather uneventful dating career, and she'd been convinced she was in love with each of them. They hadn't been in love with her. Not one. And each one left without a backwards glance, leaving her heart shattered in a million tiny pieces that took her months to put back together.

Chloe leaned back against the pool wall and crossed her arms in front of her, keeping afloat by scissoring her legs in the water. "I'm not sleeping with you again."

"You say that, but—-"

"But nothing." The smoky lust in his eyes irritated her. The answering tightness in her gut irritated her more. "I'M NOT SLEEPING WITH YOU."

"That's a shame."

She rolled her eyes. "Oh? And why is that?"

"Because we have so much fun together."

He was arrogant, extremely so, and it was obvious he lacked experience with women rejecting his advances. Every woman in the world dreamed about him, dreams that were hardly platonic. His loyal assistant probably carried an oversized black book filled with hundreds of names. He really was James Bond.

"Do you really like your martinis shaken and not stirred?" she blurted out.

"What?" He looked at her as if she'd just asked if he had three nipples, or something else just as outrageous. "Martinis? How did we get from talking about making love to cocktails?"

She lifted one shoulder. "I'm just trying to figure you out."

He cocked his head. "Oh?"

"Yeah. Is James Bond your hero?"

"The movies are fun."

"So, it's fun how he has dozens of girlfriends and drinks excessively and—"

"Plays with incredible, mind-blowing toys," he finished. "You're comparing me to a fictional character?"

"Well, if the shoe fits."

"Yes, well, I guess I'm a lot like 007."

She snapped her fingers in the water. "I thought so. After all, you chose him to impersonate at the ball."

"It's true I enjoy fancy cars and other gadgets, and I love to travel around the world to exotic locations." He slid through the water, shortening the distance between them. "But I don't have that many girlfriends. Trust me. I don't have time for it. That's why I'm doing this show. I want to find someone I can spend the rest of my life with. I want to find someone to be my bride and lifelong companion. This bachelor prince stuff is overrated."

After hearing that, Chloe wanted to throw herself against him and wrap her arms around his neck. It took all her willpower to stay against the wall and watch as he swam to her. She was almost directly beneath the waterfall now, and water splashed against her face and neck. She held her breath as he drew nearer. He stopped inches from her, his nose almost touching hers. If she reached out, she could brush his broad chest with her fingertips.

"Can I confide in you?" he asked.

"Of course," she whispered.

"I'm beginning to think this show was a ridiculous idea."

"Really?"

"Yes." He cupped her face in his hands. "I don't know what's between us, Chloe, but I want to find out. I can't confess love to you right now. I can't tell you if it's forever. I only know I've never been so affected by anyone my entire life. I know my feelings for you are deep, extremely deep, and I want nothing more than to have time to explore those feelings with you."

"But we can't," she murmured, closing her eyes and relishing the gentle caress of his fingers against her wet skin. "We can't."

"We can."

She opened her eyes and found herself looking directly into his. "What are you talking about?" Her voice was hardly even a whisper.

"We have tonight, Chloe. Let's not waste it."

The tip of his nose touched hers. One of his arms wrapped around her waist and pulled her close as his legs entwined with hers. The heat of his body was intoxicating; she loved the feel of her breasts crushed against the planes of his chest. She fanned her hands across his chest and felt the steady beat of his heart.

"I can't." She looked down at her hands and noticed they trembled. "I can't, Max. I can't put myself in that position again."

He lifted her chin with his thumb, and she gazed back into his eyes. "You can."

She shook her head and tried to pull away from him, but he held her tightly. The last thing she wanted to do was break free of his arms, but she had to in order to protect her heart.

"Let me go."

"No."

She pushed against him with the palms of her hands. When that didn't work, she balled her hands into furious fists and pounded his toned pectorals, again demanding that he release her.

"No."

"I can't do this!" she cried out hoarsely. She gazed up at him through eyes glazed with tears. "Don't make this any harder than it already is. Please. It's best if we don't do this. I need more than this. I need so much more."

"And you don't think I do?" he asked.

She stopped struggling in his arms; her hands rested on his broad shoulders, and her ankles slid enticingly against his. "What are you saying?"

"I've already told you, Chloe. I want time to explore these feelings I have for you. Frankly, the timing of our meeting sucks."

She laughed at his use of a very American term—she couldn't help herself. And she completely agreed. It did suck. Big time.

He grinned. "You agree?"

Chloe nodded. "Absolutely."

"But there isn't anything we can do about it unless we break our contracts, pay the fee, and say to hell with everyone else."

The very thought horrified her. It was unacceptable. He'd be in the headlines for a while and EVE executives would be mad at him, but eventually, because of his royal status, he'd be forgiven. *She* would not. No one gave a damn about her. She had no status, no connections, and no power to redeem herself if her name became mud in the industry.

He must've seen the horror on her face because he whispered, "I promise I'm not going to do that or demand that you do it. I understand. I'm not promising forever. I don't know if I can."

She breathed a sigh of relief. "Thank you."

"But I still think the chance might be worth it."

As he spoke, he twirled her around in the water. His right hand splayed at the small of her back; his left lingered lightly upon her hip. She circled her arms around his neck and fought the temptation to wrap her legs about his waist.

"What's your favorite color?"

His eyes widened in surprise. "What? You're full of odd questions tonight."

Chloe brushed her fingers across the base of his neck. She was quite satisfied to see him shiver at her touch.

"You did say you wanted to get to know me better. So, I thought I'd start by asking you something."

"I said I wanted to explore these incredible, amazing, wonderful feelings," he murmured huskily against her ear.

"Which includes getting to know me better. My likes and dislikes and, well, everything."

His fingers lightly touched the inside of her thigh, causing her to shudder. Hot desire turned his eyes a darker shade of blue. She tried to disentangle herself from his arms and failed miserably, only seeming to get their legs more tangled. She felt his arousal against her belly and blushed.

"Stop that." She slapped his hand away, but underwater it didn't have the same effect. Besides, her fingers lightly touched the bulge in his swim shorts, which caused a whole new cascade of shivers to shudder through her body. And his. She snatched her hand away. "Part of knowing if we have a future together is learning about each other."

His fingers stopped the playful, erotic dance on her thigh. "So, we do have a future together? You're willing to give it a chance?"

"You did say we had tonight." She pushed away from him. He let her slip through his arms. "What is your favorite color?"

"A game of questions wasn't exactly how I wanted to spend the night together," he grumbled. "I had much more exciting things in mind."

The look of crushed disappointment on his face made Chloe smile. He looked adorable. His lower lip jutted out just slightly, making him look like a small boy denied entrance into the Willy Wonka Chocolate Factory.

"Color?" she repeated.

"Brown."

"Brown?" She wrinkled her nose in distaste.

"What's wrong with brown?" He sounded offended.

"It's not a very attractive color. It's boring."

"It's my favorite."

It took her a second to realize he was studying her intently with his warm eyes. An appreciative smile lifted the corners of his mouth. She had brown hair, a shade so dark it almost looked black. And she had eyes the color of dark chocolate. She loved that her eyes could be compared to chocolate, but for years she'd wanted green or blue eyes instead of her mud-brown ones. She'd never liked the eye color until a casting director told her he thought her dark-chocolate eyes were breathtaking. She'd immediately changed her mind and decided having brown eyes wasn't bad at all; after all, she adored chocolate, especially dark chocolate. Didn't every woman?

"Is that really your favorite color?" she asked

accusingly.

"Do you think I'm lying?"

"Yes."

"Okay, I am. Brown is actually my second favorite color."

"And your favorite color is?"

"Pink!" He lunged through the water at her. She squealed and jumped out of reach of his flailing arms. "You look so sexy in that bikini."

Her pulse raced. Her heart rate accelerated. She tried to move further from him, but he was stronger and faster and a better swimmer than she was. He grabbed her around the waist and

hoisted her against him. She struggled, but her heart wasn't in it. She didn't truly mind being caught up in his arms, crushed against his body, his lips tickling her ear. He maneuvered them directly under the waterfall, and she shrieked as cold water washed down over her body.

He nuzzled her neck with his cheek. "And your favorite color is?"

She sighed happily, giving into the moment. "Pink." The intense azure of his eyes overwhelmed her. She sighed dreamily. "And blue."

His lips covered hers in a hungry kiss. She responded eagerly, opening her mouth beneath his, plunging her tongue into the hot moistness of his mouth. She never wanted to let him go. She curled her arms tighter around his neck and at last gave in to the impulse to wrap her legs about his waist. He groaned beneath her and deepened the kiss, pulling her snugly against him, both of his hands gripping the feminine curves of her backside. The waterfall's cold water continued to splash over their bodies, but Chloe hardly noticed. If anything, the slippery wetness made their embrace even more erotic.

"I thought you'd see it my way," he said against her partially opened mouth. "Women always do."

His softly mumbled words pulled her out of the passionate world she was so willing to succumb to. Chloe opened her eyes, blinking away the douse of water droplets and looking down into his upturned face. He had the gall to grin at her, an incredibly smug, self-satisfied smile that fizzled her desire and turned it into anger.

"Arrogant bastard!" she exclaimed. She unbound her legs from around his middle and pushed against him with her feet.

He sputtered in surprise. "Chloe, I—"

She gave him a good swat with her hand, and he miraculously let her go. She was completely unprepared for the sudden release and plunged into the deep end of the pool. She allowed herself to sink all the way to the bottom before pushing herself off the pebbled floor with the tips of her toes.

"What was that all about!" he shouted at her when she broke through the surface.

"You heard me. You're an arrogant bastard."

"Hey, I thought we were having a good time."

"Yeah, until you decided to go all I-am-man-hear-me-roar," she snapped, flipping long tangles of hair over her left shoulder.

He held up a hand to ward off her attack. "I confess I'm confused. You do that to me quite a lot. How did we get from kissing to this?"

She placed her hands on her hips and imitated him in a singsong voice that was most definitely not equal to his deep, timbered baritone, "I thought you'd see it my way. Women always do." She glared at him from beneath wet, clumpy lashes. Her mascara was probably running full force down her cheeks, but she didn't care. How dare he!

He looked like he was about to laugh but thought better of it. There was no mistaking the amusement in his eye. "Don't you think you're overreacting?"

"No. I'm not. You think you can have anything you want just because you're royalty. That fact doesn't give you a free pass to me."

"That's not true, and you know it. You're just picking a fight with me because it's easier."

What was he talking about? Fighting was easier? Easier than what, exactly? She continued to glare at him from the other side of the waterfall, sending telepathic messages for him to stay away from her. The problem was, she wasn't telepathic. And he started to move towards her. Damn. Shouldn't her body language tell him that moving towards her was a mad idea? She stiffened as he approached her, gliding through the water like Poseidon. He resembled a deity too. Damn him. Damn him. Damn him.

"Chloe, you're right."

She almost sank to the bottom of the pool again. "What did you say?"

He stopped directly in front of her. "I can be arrogant, but I'm not a bad guy. And I truly like you. A lot."

Chloe's anger diminished. Oh, he was so cute when he gazed at her like that. And she knew he liked her. The past two days had proved as much, hadn't they?

"Oh?" She was appalled to hear her voice sounding like a teenage girl's.

"But I'm not a bastard, certainly not. I can trace my lineage for generations, and I know I was born in wedlock. It's a documented fact—the entire world knows. So, yes, I admit to being arrogant sometimes, but I'm not a bastard."

One corner of his mouth tilted up, and she giggled. She couldn't help it. He had a way of making her laugh with just a look or one of his foolish grins.

"I apologize for the bastard part."

The other side of his mouth tilted up. "Not the arrogant part?"

"Nope. You did admit it's true."

"Sometimes I can be insufferable."

She hooted at the word. "Insufferable? It's not too often I hear that in casual conversation."

His arms coiled about her and curled her into a gentle embrace. "Now admit it."

"Admit what?" she asked innocently.

"Admit the only reason you said what you did is because you were trying to ignore your feelings for me and push me away."

Chloe lifted her chin a notch. "I was not. You really are arrogant."

"Well, *I* want to admit something."

"Confess away."

He pressed his forehead against hers; his eyes were an amazing color of blue. "I'm sorry."

"You are?"

Max nodded. He smoothed a few tendrils of wet hair away from her temples. His eyes were totally focused on her, and his fingers lingered against her skin. "I should've never said what I did. It was arrogant of me. I was an idiot. I was trying to tease you. I honestly don't know what I was thinking."

Chloe raised a hand to his face and curled a piece of his dark hair around two fingers. "I forgive you," she whispered. And she did. She wasn't mad at him any more. Maybe she had never been angry with him. Maybe she had been trying to push him away by finding something that made him less than perfect, something that gave her an excuse to end things with him, no matter how utterly stupid it was.

Max grabbed her hand and turned his lips into her palm. The feel of his mouth moving along her skin caused tentacles of fresh desire to spread through her body, and she trembled for the thousandth time.

"I'm not going to make you do anything you don't want to, Chloe. You can trust me. And I can accept not getting something I want. I've been denied things before and survived without a nasty tantrum. But I do want you. I want you more than I've ever wanted any woman. I want you to know that. You have to believe me."

"I do, Max. I believe you."

"Good."

They stared into each other's eyes for a few breathless moments. Chloe waited for him to make the next move, but he didn't; he only held her tenderly in his strong, muscled arms. They floated together, the current from the waterfall moving them about in small circles. She held his face in her hands, her fingers lightly stroking his cheeks, her thumbs caressing his lips.

"What do we do now?" he asked, his low, husky voice barely audible over the splashing of the waterfall.

She'd been waiting for him to decide, but it wasn't up to him. He was making it perfectly clear that he was giving *her* the choice. He really was the most wonderful man. And starting tomorrow, she would share him twenty-four hours a day with more than a dozen beautiful women and a camera and production crew numbering somewhere in the twenties.

There might never be another chance for them.

And how could she deny herself one last night with the man she knew, beyond a doubt, she loved? She couldn't. Tomorrow didn't matter. Only now mattered. She'd deal with the heartbreak tomorrow and the next day and the next. But now was their moment.

"Take me to bed," she whispered. She pressed her lips to his. "Make love to me, Max. Make love to me."

"I'd hoped for that. I'd so hoped for that." He returned her tentative kiss ardently. The kiss took Chloe's breath away.

"Oh, Max." She sighed softly before collapsing against him, giving herself completely to him. She laid her head on his chest and closed her eyes, loving the steady thump-thump sound of his heart.

He swept her into his arms and swam through the water, hurrying towards the shallow edge. Once there, he carried her up the steps and through the courtyard, into the foyer and up the wide flight of stairs, and finally down the hallway to her bedroom. He turned the knob and flung open the door, stepped inside, and kicked the door shut behind them.

Chloe laughed as Max tossed her onto the bed with such force the pillows bounced against the headboard and slid to the floor. She watched with wide eyes as he stripped from his swimwear, sliding the black shorts off his slim hips and down his toned thighs and calves.

Desire flamed bright in his eyes as he looked at her. "I'm going to take you fast, Chloe. I can't wait. I'm too impatient."

Intense, all-consuming warmth pooled in her middle. She knelt on the bouncy bed and unhooked the top of her bikini, removing it with one hand and dangling it in front of him, giving him an unobstructed view of her breasts. They exchanged seductive smiles before she threw the bright pink top at a nearby lamp, where it attached itself to the lampshade.

"I don't want to wait either," she told him. She stood up and slipped the bikini bottom off, twirling it with her big toe before sending it sailing it across the room, where it hit the far wall and fell into a small pink heap by the door to the walk-in closet.

Chloe couldn't believe her brashness. She had

always been a bit shy in the bedroom. But there was something about Max, something special that made him different from every man she'd ever met or had a relationship with. She didn't feel self-conscious standing before him in her birthday suit; she felt glorious and womanly and powerful. And he looked at her with so much heat in his eyes she melted inside. She wanted to share everything with him. She wanted to give him her entire self.

"Come to me," she commanded in a voice that sounded like some exotic temptress from a Greek myth. She crooked her finger at him, beckoning him to join her on the bed.

He complied, jumping onto the bed none too gracefully. He wrapped his arms around her and dragged her down onto the bed. His lips burned trails of delicious kisses up and down her arms and legs and across her belly and breasts, where the feel of his mouth enclosing her nipples sent her into a tailspin of ecstasy.

She moved her hips eagerly, encouragingly beneath him. The turbulent, delicious, soul-shattering emotions he provoked in her overwhelmed her. Tears filled her eyes and rolled down her cheeks. It was so beautiful. They were so beautiful together. This was heaven on earth.

Max placed his elbows on either side of her head, resting his weight on his arms. His fingers splayed through her hair. He looked down into her eyes...and she lost herself to him all over again. This time she lost her heart and soul. The tears continued to fall, and she bit her lower lip to keep from sobbing.

He smiled sadly. "I think I know why you cry. I know because I feel the same."

A sob escaped. He brushed the tears from her cheeks with his kisses. He showered kisses upon her, kissing her forehead, her nose, her cheeks, her lips, and the curve of her jaw. She clutched at him, holding him as close as she could. Her body strained towards his.

"Max. Max." She said his name over and over again. Ten times. Fifty times. One hundred times. She didn't know. "Love me, Max. Love me."

"Yes," he murmured against her collarbone.

He plunged deep inside her.

Chloe screamed with pleasure. She threw her head back and danced with him, matching each of his thrusts with her own. It didn't take long for her to reach her climax. It came quick and hot and shattering, exploding through her like a million fireworks on the Fourth of July. The orgasm was so intense she bit his shoulder and tasted the saltiness of blood. Her nails dug into the skin of his back. He followed her scream with one of his own, his body tensing as his orgasm ripped through his body.

Finally, he collapsed at her side and snuggled close to her. Chloe hugged him tightly, enjoying the last echoes of her orgasm.

"Wow," she let out in utter amazement.

"Wow," he agreed, kissing the crown of her head.

"You were right."

"About what?"

She waved one arm in the air, indicating their entwined bodies. "About doing this."

"You're one incredible woman, Chloe Tanner."

She traced his mouth with her fingers. "And you are one incredible man, Prince Max of Romalia. Stay with me tonight."

Max kissed her tenderly. "I can't imagine going anywhere else."

"Hmmm. Good." Chloe closed her eyes and draped a leg over his hip. "I should hate this blasted show."

"And why don't you?"

Chloe yawned. The day and their lovemaking

had exhausted her. "Because it brought us together for a little while. We wouldn't be together without it."

"But it's also keeping us apart."

"I know. That's why I should hate it." Chloe rested her head in the crook of his shoulder. He smelled so good—a scent of soap and chlorine and masculinity. His chest hairs tickled her nose.

"But I don't hate it—at least not tonight. Goodnight, my prince."

She felt his smile against her hair. "Goodnight, my lady."

Chapter Nine

Chloe curled further under the sheets. She didn't want to open her eyes. She didn't want to face the day. She preferred to stay buried under the covers, blocking out the entire world and remembering the steamy night she'd shared with Max.

Just the thought of his hands on her, his lips on her, and his body on hers made her flush. He'd been so extraordinary last night, so amazingly wonderful, and she wanted to stay in his strong arms forever. They'd made love three times in the early hours of the morning, neither getting a bit of sleep. When they weren't ravishing each other, they talked and talked and talked. She felt she'd never known a man so intimately, on so many levels.

Chloe snuggled against the pillow. She knew he was gone. He'd slipped from her bed at daybreak, placing a soft kiss on the corner of her mouth before he left. She missed him. She missed the feel of his long, muscled body next to hers. She loved how he spooned her gently against his naked body and kissed her neck and rested the palm of his hand against her belly.

She loved him.

And he could never be hers.

Chloe tossed off the covers with a strangled cry and glanced over at the alarm clock on the nightstand by her bed. It was ten o'clock. She should've been up two hours ago. The crew had probably arrived already. She couldn't remember her itinerary for the day, but she knew Max was booked the entire day. The I-want-to-be-a-princess hopefuls arrived today for a catered dinner held poolside. They would meet Max at the dinner, and *Courting His Royal Highness* would officially begin.

"I hate this," Chloe mumbled to the empty room. "I hate this, hate this, hate this!"

She felt like calling Julia, but refrained from picking up her cell phone. Communication with the outside was strictly forbidden. Secrecy enveloped the show; it was important for its success. She was surprised they hadn't snatched away her link to the outside world, but they probably would eventually. It was just a matter of time. EVE was obsessed with protecting the show's secrets from the public until it aired. Max's choice of a bride had to be a surprise for the viewers; otherwise, they wouldn't watch, and EVE's expensive endeavor would be one expensive disaster.

Chloe heard voices outside the window. She swung her legs over the side of the bed and stood up, stretching and wiggling her fingertips at the ceiling. She grabbed a silky robe, slid her feet into flip-flops, and crossed the floor to the open balcony doors. A soft breeze ruffled her tousled hair as she stepped out onto the small patio. She leaned over the railing and saw the production crew hard at work.

About a dozen people mingled below. Some set up lights, others yelled orders, and others rearranged the multitude of potted flowers and other plants that decorated the pool area. All were dressed in khaki shorts and matching blue T-shirts with *Courting His Royal Highness* emblazoned across the back.

She was disappointed not to see Max among them. She already missed his lopsided grin, the bright twinkle in his eyes, and the foreign accent of his voice. She wondered what he looked like in full royal attire. She'd only ever seen him dressed like a regular guy. To be fair, he looked better than any regular guy she'd ever seen dressed in a suit or jeans or a simple pair of dress pants, but she still wondered what he looked like attending a royal Romalian ceremony.

It dawned on her as she watched the hectic activity below that she knew absolutely nothing about his country. She knew it was a small European nation, so tiny it had about as much landmass as Rhode Island. She knew Max was due to inherit and become king as soon as his mother made the decision to relinquish the crown, which she'd held for thirty years. He had twin brothers and one sister, all of whom made headlines on a daily basis because they were single and loving it; however, they could afford to continue their single-and-free antics. Max couldn't. Not any longer, anyway. He was the oldest; therefore, it was time for him to get serious about his role as heir to Romalia, find a wife, and produce heirs to continue tradition.

Chloe crossed her arms on top of the railing and smiled as one of the frantic assistants almost fell in the pool because she was too busy jotting down directions, which one of the producers was yelling at her, in a notebook. Poor thing. She looked about ready to cry; she appeared to be about nineteen or twenty. A young thing, probably her first job.

Chloe focused her attention back on Max. She couldn't imagine the pressure of being an heir to a kingdom. Max seemed to take it all in stride. He'd been born into his position. He knew his role in life, who he was, and he accepted it.

Now, she wondered where she belonged. She wished she knew. She only knew she was always reaching, always looking, and always searching for something. She'd thought her goal was a career in the movies, but after meeting Max, she wasn't so sure. She felt safe and comfortable with him; she felt at home with him. The knowledge was at once wonderful and unsettling.

Chloe pushed away from the railing and went back into her room, where she collapsed into an oversized chair decorated in a Southwestern motif and curled her legs up underneath her. Resting her head on its back, she closed her eyes and tried a yoga-meditation technique.

She gave up after the fifth try. Her body and brain couldn't calm down long enough to relax—and she couldn't clear her mind of images of Max. He was everywhere when she closed her eyes. Blanking out and concentrating on nothing except slow, steady breathing was not going to happen this morning. She was too stressed for yoga practice, but that was why she needed it so badly. It always helped to find her center, to calm her down, and to give her the strength and positive attitude she needed to face life's challenges.

Chloe sighed and admitted defeat, standing and walking into the adjoining bathroom. She turned on the water in the gigantic shower—it could fit four people at once—and quickly brushed her teeth and gurgled with Listerine. She grimaced at the taste. Even the citrus flavor tasted like medicine and left an awful aftertaste. She secured her robe on a hook behind the bathroom door and stepped into the tiled shower surrounded on all four sides by glass doors. Wishing she had time for a nice long soak in the whirlpool tub, she cast a longing glance at it before immersing her body in the spray. Tonight she'd take a bath; she'd need it after seeing Max flirt with gorgeous women.

Her thoughts once again drifted to Max. She couldn't shake him from her mind. He was everywhere. She almost hated to wash his scent from her body; it was probably the last intimate part of him she'd ever share. She wondered what he was doing at that very moment. She wondered if he was thinking of her.

I want to go home. Chloe groaned miserably. She grabbed a bottle of shampoo, squeezed out a dime-sized dollop, and viciously began to lather her hair.

A few weeks ago, when she'd gotten the call she'd been selected to be the hostess of a new reality TV series that was sure to be a hit, she'd been ecstatic. She'd thought the doors were finally opening for her and life was about to change. Well, it had changed all right, but it didn't feel like a change for the better. Her world was topsy-turvy, and not in a good way. Nope. Not at all.

Chloe tipped her head back and rinsed the soapy suds from her dark mass of hair. As soon as the dark tresses squeaked between her fingers, she grabbed the conditioner and massaged the moisturizing balm into the ends.

She needed a game plan in order to survive the next six weeks. It would take all her willpower to push Max from her mind. She had to try and remember he was just a guy, no different than the other guys she'd dated over the years. He didn't mean anything to her. She could forget what they'd shared. She knew she could. She had to—it was the only way she would survive. It was only six weeks. It wasn't like it was a lifetime or anything.

But it felt like a lifetime.

Chloe angrily tossed a chunk of heavy hair over her shoulder and stomped her foot on the wet floor. She loved him. She loved Prince Max of Romalia, but royal princes didn't marry farm girls from Minnesota. It just didn't happen. Okay, maybe in a fairy tale, but this wasn't a fairy tale.

"I'm no princess in disguise," Chloe murmured woefully. "There's no happy ending for me."

But those women competing for a chance to be his bride weren't members of the royalty either.

"That's right!" Chloe crowed happily. Her happiness quickly vanished. Although it was comforting to know Max didn't care if he married a woman with royal blood or not, she still didn't have a chance in hell at becoming his bride.

She tried to wash Max from her mind by reaching for a bar of soap and quickly covering her entire body with scented fragrance. It smelled of apples and cinnamon. She loved it. It was homemade soap created by an elderly lady in her hometown. She ordered bars by the dozen. The trendy, posh, and outlandishly expensive boutiques in Los Angeles sold dozens of designer lotions and bath products, but they couldn't compete with Apple Orchard Heaven. It was her signature fragrance.

Chloe rinsed with lightening speed. She dried off with an oversized white towel, wrapped it about her body, and hurried back into the bedroom. She was rummaging through the walk-in closet, trying to decide what to wear, when she heard a knock at the door.

"Just a minute."

"Miss Tanner, you're needed downstairs immediately. The director wants to discuss some things with you and with Prince Max about what's happening today on set."

Chloe pulled on lacy pink panties and a matching bra. Over the lingerie, she tugged on a pink tank top and pair of jean shorts. She picked up a comb on the way to the door, dragging it through her mass of hair—conditioner barely helped—and pulled open the door. A wide-eyed assistant stood in the hallway with a large smile plastered on his face and a clipboard in his hands.

"Good morning, Miss Tanner."

"Good morning," she said, returning his smile.

"I have your itinerary here." He unclipped a wad of papers and handed the pile to her.

"Thanks." Chloe didn't have the heart to remind him she already had a complete itinerary still packed in her suitcase. "They want me now?"

The assistant glanced at his clipboard and nodded. "Yes, immediately. I'm sorry I didn't get the itinerary to you sooner." He swallowed hard and looked back at her. "I hope I don't lose my job over this."

Chloe patted his shoulder sympathetically. "I doubt that. No harm done. You can blame it on me."

"But you didn't have a schedule. I can't do that."

She shrugged. It was sort of her fault; after all, she hadn't bothered to look at her schedule for the past two days. She'd been too distracted by Max. Much too distracted.

"Don't worry about it. I give you permission to tell the producers it's all my fault."

The expression on his face was a mixture of horror and relief. "Thanks a lot. But I feel kind of bad doing that."

"Well, I'm not late yet, am I?"

He shook his head.

"How much time do I have?"

"Fifteen minutes."

She raised an eyebrow. "I thought you said I was needed immediately?"

He flushed. "Sorry about that."

She leaned forward and said in a secretive whisper, "Well, fifteen minutes means immediately for a woman. We need lots of time to look gorgeous, you know. I'm hardly ready for a close-up. I just got out of the shower."

He grinned, blushed a shade deeper, and eyed her appreciatively. "You look pretty to me."

"Thanks."

"I better get going." He turned away and started walking down the hall.

"What's your name?" she called.

He stopped and looked back over his shoulder. "Jordan."

"Nice to meet you, Jordan."

"You too, Miss Tanner."

"I sound so old when you call me that. Call me Chloe."

"Okay." He grinned from ear to ear. "It's nice to meet you, Chloe."

Chloe watched him vanish around the corner before stepping back into the bedroom. She didn't bother to shut the door and plopped down on the bed, removing the last of the snarls from her hair. When she was satisfied her hair was not a tangled mass any longer, she tossed the wide-tooth comb on the unmade bed and decided it was time to face the day. Wardrobe and makeup would take care of her appearance. She had no doubt she'd look like a million bucks by the time the cameras rolled. An ugly duckling could look like a swan with the right people helping her, beauty products, and digital touch-ups.

She took a deep breath, gave herself a mental pep talk, and exited the room, securing the door firmly behind her. She was happy at the prospect of seeing Max again, but not at all thrilled about the circumstances. It would be all business now. The kisses and passionate encounters and tender words were over. That was just the way it was.

****

Max patiently listened while Jack Parker, the show's executive producer and director, discussed the day's shoot with him. He really wasn't interested. His mind was on Chloe; it had been on Chloe the entire morning. He missed her. It had taken all his willpower to pull himself from her. She'd looked so adorable snuggled close against him, a sleepy smile on her lips, one hand tucked under her cheek. He'd wanted to wake her again and make love to her and cuddle with her all day under the tumbled sheets.

But duty called. Duty always called.

"You'll meet the girls as they arrive. After they settle in to their assigned rooms, they will meet you for dinner by the pool," Mr. Parker said as he typed frantically on a laptop computer.

Max nodded. He'd never met anyone as hyper as Jack. The guy was a continuous ball of energy. Either nature had gifted him with it, or it could be attributed to the six cups of hazelnut coffee he'd gulped down since he arrived two hours ago. The guy's hands were actually shaking. Max smiled. And he'd thought Eric was bad.

No one completed more in a day than Eric, but without his planner he was absolutely lost. Max had seen it happen. Two years ago, as a joke, he'd purposely misplaced the oversized black planner glued to Eric's side. Eric went into fits, hyperventilated, and almost called out Max's complete security guard to find it. He hadn't been too happy to find it was a joke and had given Max the cold shoulder for almost an entire week.

"Do you know when Eric arrives?" Max asked.

Mr. Parker stopped talking and typing and glanced up from his keyboard. "Who?"

"Mr. Von Stratton."

"Mr. Von Stratton should arrive any minute." He went back to spewing forth information about the day and coming week and yelling at his assistant for another cup of coffee.

"Do you really think you need another cup of coffee?" Max asked.

"Yes. If I don't have my coffee, I can't function."

Max believed it. As the assistant raced past him to fulfill the eccentric director's request, Max mouthed "make it decaf." She started to laugh, but clapped her hand over her mouth to smother the giggles. Mr. Parker didn't seem to notice. He was far too busy being a Nazi general and giving Max orders about how he was supposed to act and what he was supposed to do.

Max's mind drifted again to Chloe and the night they'd shared. Desire bloomed anew at the thought of her. What was he doing? He should break the contract with EVE, pay a huge fine to make amends, and sweep Chloe off her feet and into his arms forever. There was no reason why he couldn't: after all, he was the Prince of Romalia. What was the use of having all that power and prestige if he couldn't use it to his advantage?

Breaking a contract might taint his family honor for a while, but the world was forgiving to its royals. However, Chloe was relying on this to propel her struggling career. Her eyes lighted up when she talked about being an actress. How could he destroy her dream just because he desired her? And he couldn't promise her a happily forever after. Or could he?

Do I love her? Maybe. I just don't know.

He knew with certainty he'd never felt this way about any woman before, and he'd dated quite a few; Eric surely had a number somewhere in one of his organizers. Chloe made him happy. Thinking about her made him smile. Being with her made him feel whole. Was that love? He was starting to think so. He couldn't get enough of her, and she was becoming important to him—he couldn't imagine life without her.

"And that will conclude the week," Mr. Parker interrupted Max's thoughts. He glanced up from the computer screen and scanned the room. "I wonder where Miss Tanner is? She's going to be late in two minutes. And you're needed elsewhere."

Damn. The show. He'd thought the show was such a good idea at first, but now he didn't want anything to do with it. He wanted out. He wasn't interested in any woman other than Chloe, and she wasn't one of the choices on *Courting His Royal Highness*. Something had to be done. And he knew it was up to him to do it.

"And where am I supposed to be?" Max asked.

Mr. Parker looked completely and utterly exasperated. "Makeup and wardrobe. Haven't you been listening to me? And it's on your schedule. Don't you look at that thing?"

Max shook his head. "I usually have Eric to do that." It was a true statement. Eric scheduled everything for him and was always around to inform him of where he should be and when.

Jack guffawed. "Royalty!"

"Hey!" Max snapped irritably. He didn't appreciate the attitude. Okay, okay, so he was a little spoiled and pampered. It didn't mean he was incompetent. He simply didn't have the experience of organizing and scheduling his life. That job had always belonged to Romalia officials and Eric. It was just the way things were. Period.

"Ah, there's Sleeping Beauty. So, you finally decided to join us."

Max turned his focus from clobbering Mr. Parker with his laptop to the love of his life. Chloe stood in the doorway to the living room. She was a vision in a pink tank top and denim shorts, which showed off her legs to perfection. Pink had to be one of her favorite colors. It was something he planned to remember for future reference. Pink roses, pink lingerie, pink champagne, pink....

"Sorry if I'm late, Mr. Parker."

"Don't worry about it, kid." Mr. Parker waved off her apology with one hand. "You're not late at all. It's just that I start everything early. Remember that for future reference."

Chloe smiled her lovely smile. "Okay."

Suddenly, Max realized he *did* love Chloe Tanner. He loved her completely and madly and deeply. He loved her as a man was supposed to love a woman. He wanted a future with her. He wanted her to be his bride, his princess, his wife, and his queen. He wanted to have children with her, children with her large brown eyes and dark wavy hair.

The realization hit him like a bolt of lightening. He was shocked by it, and yet he was not. It was simple. He saw things clearly, as he never had before. He'd found his soul mate. He'd found his other half. And he was going to do everything and anything to keep her in his life.

But did she love him?

He knew she cared for him. He could see it in her chocolate eyes. But love? He didn't know. He'd only just realized he loved her. Maybe she *did* love him, but didn't even know it yet. He had to convince her they were meant to be together. He had to show her how much he loved her.

Max wanted to bolt from his chair, cross the room, and kiss her. She looked so cute. He wanted to kiss her all day long and all night and all week and all year.

"Where's my cup of coffee!" Mr. Parker yelled.

His assistant scurried in with a steaming cup.

"Coffee, Miss Tanner?"

"Tea, please."

"Get Miss Tanner some tea."

"Yes, sir." The assistant exited the room as fast as she could.

Mr. Parker gestured to an empty seat. "Sit down. Sit down. Join us. We've got much to discuss. I'm afraid Max can't stay. I've already filled him in. He seems to be oblivious to what's on the menu today and all week. Doesn't look at his schedule, I guess."

"It's with Eric."

"Ah, yes, Mr. Von Stratton."

"I'll admit I haven't looked at mine either."

Mr. Parker groaned. "What am I going to do with you two? My two stars don't have a clue what they're supposed to do. What did you do the last couple of days?"

Max grinned at Chloe. She grinned back. They'd definitely had other things on their minds. He was happy to hear she hadn't given too much thought to her schedule either. He hoped she'd been focusing on him—and there was something warm and honeyed in her eyes that told him she had. She wasn't looking at Mr. Parker, hadn't glanced at him once. She had eyes only for Max. And he had eyes only for her.

"Sit down, Miss Tanner. We've got a lot to cover in not a lot of time." Mr. Parker took a quick sip of his coffee. He grimaced. "Not hot enough. And not enough cream. Max, you're already off schedule. Get going."

Max stood at the same time as Chloe crossed the distance between them. He touched her arm. She gazed up into his eyes. He wanted to tell her right then and there that he loved her. He loved her so much that he couldn't imagine life without her. She was his life. But this wasn't the moment to tell her—not in front of their executive producer and director.

"Did you sleep well?" he asked softly.

She blushed. It made her more beautiful. He lightly squeezed her wrist. "I did. Very well," she whispered.

"Me, too," he whispered back.

"I'm glad you're both well-rested," Mr. Parker chimed in. "Now let's get to work."

"I'll see you soon?" And he didn't mean in the company of others.

"I hope so," she said softly. She covered his hand with hers briefly. "I'd like that." He saw sadness cloud her eyes. "But I don't know how that's possible, Max."

"Good grief! You're going to see each other every day for the next six weeks!" exclaimed Mr. Parker with a shake of his head. He took another sip of his coffee and complained once again, very loudly, that it wasn't hot enough.

"I need to talk to you, Chloe."

"There's nothing to talk about."

"There is."

She shook her head and pulled gently away from him. "No. There's nothing to talk about. We have a job to do. Let's do it as professionally as we can."

"But there's so much to say, Chloe. I have so much to tell you. You have no idea."

The despair in her smile wrenched his heart. "No. It's over. It's over," she murmured softly so Mr. Parker couldn't hear. "It was wonderful. But it's done. Finished. Let's not continue to torture ourselves."

He was about to confess his love to her, but Mr. Parker interrupted him, informing Max—quite authoritatively—that he was needed immediately in makeup and wardrobe. Chloe turned away from him, sinking into an overstuffed chair and giving her complete attention to Mr. Parker, who immediately launched into informing her about her duties for the day.

Max was not used to being dismissed. He usually dismissed people. But it was obvious Mr. Parker was finished with him, and Chloe didn't want to talk about what was happening between them.

Max had never been so frustrated. He felt helpless. A tide of events had been set in motion— thanks to him—and there seemed to be nothing he could do to stop it. He reluctantly left the room. As he did so, he was tempted to stomp from the room like a little boy, but refrained. That was not an attractive quality in a grown man.

What was he going to do? There had to be some way to stop this crazy, seemingly uncontrollable ride he was on. He was a prince. He had oodles of people at his disposal. There had to be something he could do to flip the tables in his favor.

Chapter Ten

Weeks from hell. That was what the last three weeks had been. Chloe had hated every second of every minute of every day within those three weeks. Watching the prospective brides swarm over Max was enough to drive her insane. And watching him plaster that amazing I'm-a-prince-so-love-me smile on his handsome face made her absolutely nauseated. Sometimes she almost believed he enjoyed every moment with these complete strangers.

But what man wouldn't have a fabulous time? After all, the fifteen women were absolutely gorgeous. And they weren't flakes either. Of the six who remained, there were a non-profit lawyer, a pediatric doctor, a high-school history teacher, a college English instructor, a zoologist, and a motivational speaker and etiquette specialist. Just perfect.

Chloe felt inadequate compared to each one. Antonia and Lester had done a fantastic job with their selections. Each woman acted as if she could marry a prince and slip into the role of princess effortlessly. Chloe envied them. She hated that she did, but she wanted to be one of Max's choices. She wanted it badly. And she hated helping him choose which women to keep each week. It was horribly hard sitting with him and going over attributes and flaws, of which there were very few; in fact, she was pretty sure she knew who the two finalists would be. But even that she could bear with dignity.

What she had a hard time dealing with was that

it seemed as if Max was actually interested in the women. It felt like he'd completely lost interest in her. She tried not to judge him too harshly. First of all, she'd told him to forget about what they'd shared. Secondly, they hadn't been alone since the night they'd made love. When they were together, they weren't really together. The cameras were always rolling, and they always had an audience.

Oh, they'd been together plenty. Their days were filled with meetings and more meetings. She had meetings with makeup, hair, and wardrobe, and producers, directors, and camera operators. She was so sick of people in her business twenty-four hours a day, she was about ready to pull her hair out. She was surprised the people with the white jackets hadn't arrived to take her away. She'd almost prefer a sanitarium to the lunacy of *Courting His Royal Highness.*

She wanted out. And there was no way out.

Chloe sank deeper into the tub and closed her eyes. She tried very hard not to think of Max, but it was next to impossible. He haunted her whenever she was alone. His blue eyes, his dark hair, his wonderful dimples, his fantastic build, the way he wiggled his eyebrows when he was amused, the way his smile filled an entire room.

She missed his smile—his *real* smile. The one he'd bestowed upon her when they'd been alone together those two brief days.

Chloe brushed a tear from her cheek with shaking fingers. What she needed was a good cry, but she didn't have time to unleash her shattered emotions. She felt alone and lost and, well, so alone. It was a horrible, terrible, miserable feeling. And her heart ached. It ached so badly.

Another tear slid down her cheek. She ignored it, deciding maybe it was best to not fight it anymore. She'd held it inside for three long, excruciating, tortuous weeks.

"Max," she whispered softly into the stillness of the bathroom. "I miss you. I miss you more than I ever thought possible."

Bubbles popped and crackled near her ears. She sank deeper into the water, immersing herself in the fragrant bath. She pressed the button for the jets and sighed as the water started to swirl about her emotionally and physically drained body.

"Three more weeks." She could do this for three more weeks. And then she'd be free of Max forever. "Three more weeks."

Chloe wasn't normally a crier. It took a lot to bring her to tears. But she couldn't stop the tears any longer. They cascaded down her cheeks; faster and faster they fell, dripping off her chin and nose into the water.

Chloe couldn't remember the last time she'd suffered a broken heart. It had been awhile. Her last great love had been a boy in high school. Gregory Adams. She'd been madly, deeply, totally in love with him. But he broke her heart senior year. She'd caught him cheating on her with her cousin and best friend, Daisy. That heartache propelled her to pack up her bags after graduation and move to California.

Gregory and Daisy had married a year after high school. Daisy owned a beauty salon—gossip central—in their small town, and Gregory worked as the assistant football coach to the high-school football team—his dream job. They happened to be the IT couple of the town.

And for some odd reason, at that moment, Chloe missed them dreadfully.

Weird.

Chloe sighed sadly and grabbed a mesh sponge. She only hoped the sacrifices she was making with her heart would pay off in the end. Perhaps if she gained her fame and fortune, she would forget about the Gregory's and Max's of the world and be able to concentrate on her career.

She smiled. She envisioned herself winning and accepting the Academy Award, placing her handprints in the cement in front of Grauman's Chinese Theater. She also wanted to use her celebrity status to help thousands of less fortunate people across the world and donate millions to arts programs in schools across the country. She always thought is so sad that the arts and music programs were usually the first to get cut when budgets were tight.

Chloe focused on her dreams. They improved her mood, minimized the ache in her heart, and stopped the tears. She needed a different focus. Focusing on Max only made her incredibly sad. And she didn't want to be sad. Everyone wanted to be happy, and she was no different.

"Chloe?"

Her eyes snapped open. Her entire body stiffened. The good feelings and pleasant dreams drifted away. She found herself looking directly into a pair of brilliant blue eyes framed by long, black lashes. His eyes. And his dimpled smile. And his beautiful face.

"What are you doing in here?" she asked, completely and totally startled by his appearance in her bathroom.

He filled the entire doorway of the room with his tall frame, looking good enough to eat in loose-fitting jeans and a red T-shirt. He was barefoot, which was incredibly sexy, and his hair was damp. The midnight tendrils of hair curled attractively against the curves of his ears and at the nape of his neck.

Chloe's insides tingled. Her heart tripped. Her pulse quickened.

"The door was locked."

His blue eyes caressed her face. "I have a key."

Her eyes widened. "Excuse me?"

He looked guilty, ashamedly so. "I had it made."

"You had it made?" she asked incredulously.

"Do you forgive me?"

"I think it's rather pompous of you to do so without asking me," she retorted. "Give me the key and get out of my room. Now."

"No."

Chloe sat up so fast that water sloshed over the sides. Hot anger seared through her. She had to be angry with him—it was her only defense against his irresistible charisma, and she refused to be a victim again. Once was enough. Okay, twice. But she couldn't afford to give in to him again. Her heart wouldn't survive another encounter.

She realized her abrupt rise from the tub exposed her breasts. She clasped her hands over them and glared hatefully at him, sinking back into the water.

He smiled at her. His eyes twinkled. "It isn't like I haven't seen you naked before."

She pointed at him, her forefinger shaking angrily. "Don't you dare! Don't you dare bring up our past history! Not ever!" She slapped the water. "Get out! Get out! Get out! Can't I have a moment alone?"

His smile vanished, as did the twinkling of his eyes, but he didn't leave. He walked further into the room. Chloe glared at him. All her defenses were up. She was armed for battle. She knew what her priorities were now—and he was not among them.

"What do you think you're doing?" she demanded, crossing her arms over her chest and praying the overdose of bubbles wouldn't vanish and expose her entire body to his view.

"I wanted to talk to you. It's been so long since we've been alone."

Chloe looked away from his searching gaze. "I don't want you here, Your Highness."

He stopped his approach, coming to a standstill in the middle of the room. She looked up at him, and her heart lurched. Pain darkened his eyes. She couldn't bear it. She glanced away again and willed herself to be strong. She would not hand over her body or her heart to him. Never again. Never again. Nothing could come of it. No happily-ever-after existed for them.

"Chloe, my feelings for you haven't changed."

"What feelings are those?" she asked softly.

He kneeled beside the tub. "You know what feelings."

"No." She moved as far away as she could from him, which wasn't much, and focused her attention on the tiled wall. "Lust? Passion?"

"I've missed you." He placed a gentle hand on her shoulder. "I need you."

The feel of his hand on her skin sent warm shivers through her body. Her body betrayed her. Anger and frustration overflowed inside her.

"You seem very happy courting those women."

Silence filled the small space between them. She wished he would leave. Oh, how she wished he would leave.

"Please look at me."

She shook her head. "No. I can't."

"Why?"

"Because."

"Because why?"

She shrugged. "Just because."

"I'm playing a part."

Chloe turned sharply. Her eyes met his. "Well, then, you're doing a very convincing job. Congratulations. Perhaps you'll win an Emmy," she snapped sarcastically.

"We knew this would be difficult."

"Difficult?" She laughed. "Difficult? Is that all this is to you?"

His gaze held hers. "No. It's worse than that."

"Could you please get my robe?"

Max nodded. He stood, unhooked the flowered terrycloth robe from the wall, and held it out to her. She stepped out of the tub and gladly slipped into the soft robe, tying the belt tight around her waist before turning to face him.

"There's nothing to talk about, Max. We accepted this."

"But you're so angry with me. I see it every day, and it tears me apart."

"You're worried about me?"

"Yes."

"It took you three weeks to come talk to me. That's how worried you are about me?"

He hung his head. "I'm sorry about that. I truly am. They've had me doing—"

"I know, Max. I know."

They stared at each other. Unspoken words and emotional tension spanned the distance between them. Chloe wanted to throw herself in his arms. She wanted to press her lips against his. She wanted to be loved and to love him. But she couldn't. They couldn't.

"Please leave, Max. It's okay. I'm okay. I've accepted that you'd rather have one of them than me."

He grabbed her elbow as she stepped past him and pulled her against him. "I can't do this anymore. I can't pretend as if there is nothing between us."

"There isn't anything, Max. There isn't." She tried to be brave. She tried to smile, but she failed. Her lips trembled. Tears blurred her eyes. "We made our bed."

"I can't forget what we shared. How can you?" Chloe didn't think it possible for her heart to break all over again. But she was wrong. She lifted a hand to his cheek. "I'll treasure it always, but we can't be together. You know that."

"I don't care about them," he whispered hoarsely. He brushed his lips against her palm. "I don't feel the same for them as I do for you."

"Oh, Max."

He grasped her hand and held it tenderly between both of his. He kissed her fingertips so lovingly that Chloe almost cried. "Just tell me one thing, Chloe."

"What's the one thing?"

"Have your feelings for me changed?"

She shook her head. She couldn't lie to him. "No. My feelings for you haven't changed." He smiled down at her. She grinned up at him. "But why does that matter, Max?"

"It matters. Trust me. It matters." He kissed each one of her fingertips. "Everything is going to work out, Chloe. Trust me."

She did trust him. But she didn't know how he could make this right. They were contracted to the show. And she needed the show. She'd explained that to him. She needed the job. He didn't, but she did. And she couldn't give it all up. She had to be sure they had a forever, and she wasn't—he had yet to confess his love to her. He had yet to promise forever. She did love him. Her entire body and heart and mind told her so. But did he love her?

He cared deeply for her. His eyes reflected the sincerity of his feelings. But he had yet to utter the words, those wonderful three little words that meant so much to a girl like her. And it would be even better if "I love you" was followed by "Will you marry me?" Yes, that was what she wanted. She wouldn't accept anything but marriage from Prince Max of Romalia. She deserved that commitment. She deserved happily-ever-after with Max. Anything less, and she'd be cheating herself and her heart.

"Please go. I need you to go."

"I'll go." He kissed her forehead and then her nose and then the corner of her mouth. She let him because she loved him, and it felt so good to be close to him after so long being away.

"Can I trust you to not come back into my room uninvited?" she asked softly.

He nodded. "Can I trust you to believe in me when I say there is hope for us and everything will work out?"

"Max—"

He silenced her with a quick kiss. "Don't forget who I am, Miss Chloe Tanner."

"I'm not."

"I'm used to getting everything I want."

Chloe pushed a curl behind his ear. "Yeah, so you've told me."

"And I want you."

"No one gets everything they want, Max. I think it's about time you learned that."

He revealed his dimples in her special smile, the smile only meant for her. She almost swooned into his arms. That smile was her undoing. She couldn't resist it.

"Never underestimate the power of Crown Prince Max of Romalia." He brushed his lips against her cheek. "Just don't be mad with me anymore. Please."

She laughed. She couldn't help it—he sounded like a little boy. "I'll try not to be angry at you. I'll try very hard."

He tweaked her nose. "Good. We have a meeting first thing in the morning."

"We do?" That was news to her. She didn't remember having a meeting scheduled tomorrow morning. She raised an eyebrow at him. "Truly?"

"Yep. We're going for a walk in the desert."

"What?"

"You and me."

"Alone?"

His smile deepened. Those dimples were extra adorable; he looked positively happy with himself. "Yes, alone."

"Impossible."

He winked. "Nothing is impossible, darling. Nothing at all."

"Especially for a prince?"

"Especially for a prince."

"You are arrogant."

"But I'm also irresistibly charming."

She giggled. "That to."

"Tomorrow morning? Sunrise?"

"I suppose. Are you sure we'll be alone?"

"Yep." He exited the bathroom. She followed behind, marveling at the skip in his step. He seemed very, very ecstatic about something.

"What's going on?"

"I need your help with something."

"Help you with what?" she asked curiously.

"Tomorrow. You'll find out tomorrow." He turned in the doorway, grinning from ear to ear. "Good night."

"Good night, Max."

Chloe leaned against the doorframe and watched him hurry down the hallway. What on earth was he up to? Alone together? How was that even possible? They couldn't leave the estate, and the movie cameras and EVE personnel watched their every move, not to mention the bombshells sleeping peacefully in the other wing of the house and dreaming of becoming the next Romalian princess.

She pulled the door closed and flipped the lock. For a moment she leaned against the wide door, her forehead pressed against the cool wood. She tried to take deep breaths, tried to calm the erratic beating of her heart. She was so close to risking everything for him. She loved a guy who had yet to admit his love for her.

But I haven't told him how I truly feel either.

She ignored the little voice inside her head and decided it was time to involve a third party, someone who could be objective and give her advice. She needed advice. She needed it very badly.

Chloe opened the top drawer of the nightstand, rummaged through her Kate Spade purse, and pulled out her bright pink cell phone. She was going to call Jules. She knew she wasn't supposed to have contact with the world outside this mansion, at least not for another few weeks, but she needed to talk to someone. Besides, Julia already knew about Max and the show.

But she didn't know Chloe was in love with the star of *Courting His Royal Highness*. She was about to find out.

Julia answered on the first ring. "Omigod! What are you doing calling me? I thought that was forbidden."

Chloe had never been so thankful to hear her friend's bubbly voice. She clutched the phone tightly and sank onto the bed. "It is."

"Am I hearing this right? Chloe Tanner is breaking the rules. Golly. Is this my best friend?"

"I just had to talk to you, Jules. I miss you."

"I miss you, too. The City of Angels isn't the same without you, Chloe."

"How's Domino?"

"Great. Fantastic. He sleeps all day and all night. But he's alive. I can assure you of that."

"Give him a kiss for me."

"Done. So, what's up? I know you love your cat, but I don't think that's why you're calling me."

"This is so much harder than I thought," Chloe sighed miserably into the phone. "I didn't expect it to be this hard."

Amy Hahn

"You want him, don't you?"

"Yes. You have no idea how much." Chloe curled up onto her side, hugging a pillow to her chest.

"I have a solution for you."

"What?"

"Sleep with the guy. Get it out of your system. Think of the story you could tell your grandchildren someday. Having sex with the Prince of Romalia."

"Julia!" Chloe didn't think she really wanted to sit around telling stories about her sexual escapades to her grandchildren.

Julia laughed. "What would it hurt? After all, after this you'll never see him again. He'll be out of your life forever, married to one of the dumb girls on that ridiculous show."

"That's the problem. I don't want him to be out of my life forever. I want him in my life forever."

Silence greeted Chloe on the other end of the phone.

"What did you say?"

"I said—"

"I know what you said. You love the guy. Gosh, Chloe, you're in love with a man who, according to you, is completely off-limits. This has absolutely nothing to do with sex and everything to do with your tender heart. Have you completely and totally lost your mind?"

"Yes!" Chloe shouted into the phone. "More so my heart."

"Don't sleep with him then. It'll only make things worse."

Chloe buried her face in the pillow. "I already did," she squeaked into the phone.

Julia squawked. "What? Where? When?"

"At EVE's Halloween Ball."

"I can't believe this. Are you telling me my best friend, cautious Chloe, had a one-night stand with the Prince of Romalia and didn't tell me?"

156

Chloe grimaced. "Yes. But in my defense, I didn't know it was him."

"Didn't know!" shrieked Julia. "How did you not know it was one of the most famous bachelors in the world?"

"Do I really need to answer that?" Chloe held the phone away from her ear and glowered at it for a second. Julia knew full well she didn't know much about royalty. Actors, yes, but royal princes? Most definitely no.

"But you've never done something like that before. That sounds like something I'd do. I must say I'm impressed."

"Don't be."

"And now you're in love."

"Madly."

"Was he good?"

"Good?"

"In bed."

"Jules!"

"Okay, okay, but was he?"

Chloe smiled warmly, remembering what it was like to spend a night in his arms, to hear his deep voice whispering words of love and devotion in her ear, to feel his lips and hands caress her skin. Yes, he was good. But it was more than that. They were good *together*.

"Chloe. Talk. Now."

"Amazing. I can't even describe it. It was incredible."

"I knew it! No one could look that good and be bad in bed. It'd be a shameful waste. Simply shameful."

"What do I do, Jules? I'm in love with a guy I can't have."

"Who said that? You?"

Chloe held the phone away from her and glared at it. She wished she could wring her best friend's neck. "The show!"

"Minor detail."

"Minor detail?"

"Yep. Now, has he told you he loves you?"

"No. That's why I can't wait for this to be over. It's torture. I don't know if he loves me or not. I know he's attracted to me, I know we have chemistry—but does that equal love?"

"If you feel there's something with Prince Max, then you should fight for it."

"But—"

"Don't give me mumble-jumble about your career and all that nonsense." Julia knew her well—probably too well. "Tell him how you feel. He might feel the same. Take a chance on love, Chloe. If you don't, then you're never going to be happy. Do you think money and fame bring happiness?"

The statement offended Chloe. She flopped over onto her back and stared at the ceiling. "I'm not that shallow. You know me better than that."

"Yes, but you've been so focused on being successful, you've pushed love aside. I say you should go for it."

"But—"

"But nothing. So it might not work out. Big deal. That's life, but at least you took the chance."

"I'm scared."

"Of course you are."

"You should see the girls he has to choose from."

"Gorgeous?"

"And smart."

"So are you. Don't forget that. You'd make a great princess. Can I be your assistant?"

Chloe laughed. Julia always brightened her mood. "I couldn't do it without you."

"So, are you going to tell him?"

Chloe's somber mood returned. She didn't dare tell him her true feelings. What if he didn't return them? She didn't want to be another woman in his long list of attractive conquests. "I don't think I can."

"You can. I know you can."

"And then what?"

"You'll have fun."

"And then what?"

"Hopefully, you'll walk down the aisle and become a princess."

"Do you honestly believe that?"

"Doesn't every little girl?" Chloe heard the tender smile in Julia's voice. "Go for it."

"He wants to meet me tomorrow at sunrise. He says he needs my help with something."

"Hmmm. I think that's good. You'll be alone?"

"Yes."

"A perfect time to tell him how you really feel."

"But—"

"Chloe."

"All right. I'll tell him."

"Tell me about your competition."

"I'm beginning to regret calling you."

"No you're not. Tell me about them, and I'll reassure you they've got nothing on you."

"Thanks, Jules."

"No problem. Isn't that what friends are for?"

Chloe was very thankful to have a friend like Julia. She always helped put things into perspective. She took chances and seldom thought about the consequences. Julia was the complete opposite of Chloe; they balanced each other well. Chloe needed a little more of Julia's so-who-cares-what-happens attitude in order to confess her love for Max. She didn't know if she could do it—but she hoped so.

Chapter Eleven

Shades of pink and orange and yellow streaked the horizon as Chloe followed Max on a zig-zaggy path up the side of the McDowell Mountains, enjoying the view of his adorable backside more than the breathtaking view of a Sonoran Desert sunrise. He was dressed in navy shorts—which provided a great view of his long legs—and a white T-shirt that stretched quite attractively across his muscled chest.

The sleeping beauties back at the mansion had no idea what they were missing.

Chloe was thankful for a few minutes alone with Max. It was nice to be away from the cameras and the production crew and Mr. Parker with his caffeine high—and especially those *women*.

Max glanced over his shoulder and smiled. Chloe grinned back. Gosh, he was gorgeous. No wonder he was a favorite subject of the infamous paparazzi. And those eyes....Wow! Extraordinary. Only Paul Newman had eyes as blue. And right at that moment, those eyes were focused completely and totally on her.

"So, are you going to tell me what we're doing out here?" she asked as she avoided a rolling tumbleweed. "Weren't you going to ask me about something? You wanted my help?"

"All in good time, my dear. All in good time."

Chloe tossed him a quizzical glance. "Why are you being so secretive?" She looked around her. "Am I on camera?"

"Nope. Not at the moment."

"Okay, so it's only a matter of time before the

camera crew shows up and starts rolling."

"Not this morning." He glanced down at his watch. "They'll probably just be starting to set up for the day."

"What about Mr. Von Stratton? Won't he wonder where you've run off to?"

Max shook his dark head. "He's still in bed. At least for another thirty minutes or so."

Chloe really wanted to run her fingers through the inky black tendrils. Could a man be any more perfect? She didn't think so. How could she possibly give him up without a fight?

Julia was right—she couldn't just let him go. She had to take a chance that whatever existed between them was more than intense attraction. He had to feel it as well, didn't he?

"So, what did you want from me, Max?"

"Not yet. I want to enjoy this moment."

Chloe stopped her ascent up the steep incline, leaned against an oversized boulder and took a deep breath. She was definitely out of shape. She couldn't remember the last time she'd really exercised. "Can we rest a bit?"

"Can't you keep up with me?"

"You're not winded at all?"

He shook his dark head. His blue eyes twinkled. "Nope. I work out on a regular basis."

Chloe released an exhausted sigh. "And how do you find time for that?"

"Eric schedules it in for me," he said with a wink. "Having a personal assistant does have its advantages."

"I can see that. I'm impressed."

Max puffed out his chest. "Why, thank you. However, it looks like you need some improvement."

She swatted his arm and scowled. "Not funny. Not funny at all. I'm just a little out of shape."

He cocked his head to one side and raised an

eyebrow. "Really? Just a little?"

She laughed and swatted his arm again. "Knock it off. I just haven't put exercising at the top of my list of things to do."

"You should."

"Don't give me a lecture. I know I'm bad. Once I get into a routine, I do very well, but I've been too busy lately to worry about fitting it in."

"Well, at least you look great, Chloe. You look absolutely beautiful—especially right now."

She felt her face flush a brilliant red. "Stop that. Don't say things you don't mean."

"But I do mean it, Chloe. I wouldn't lie about something this important. You're beautiful. And that's not an opinion. It's the honest truth."

Chloe stared into his blue eyes and lost her heart and soul all over again. How did he do it? How did he make her feel like a princess? How did he make her feel as if she were the most important person in his world?

"I betcha you say that to all the girls," she whispered.

He inched closer. "I *betcha* I don't," he whispered back as his hands grasped hers gently. His fingers curled around the small circumference of each wrist, and the slow caress of his fingertips caused goose bumps to pop up and down her arms.

"I'm planning on watching the dates you've had with these prospective princesses," she murmured softly, her eyes never leaving his. His eyes were magnetic; they lured her in. She could stare into the blue depths all day long.

"Why?"

"Just to see for myself if you say the same things to all the girls you're attracted to."

His body brushed up against hers. "I can assure you that I do not. You get special treatment from me. Only you."

Her heart thump-thumped with pleasure at his words. "I don't know if I can believe you."

"Then watch for yourself." His arm snaked about her middle, and he drew her slowly up against his solid form. "I wouldn't lie to you. I promise I'll never lie to you."

She shivered in his arms, despite the heat of the morning sun rising behind her in the Arizona sky. She could feel the warmth of it against her back; she saw its light in the sapphire blue of his eyes. Chloe touched the palms of her hands to his bare forearms, making small circles with the tips of her fingers on his sun-kissed skin.

"Why are we here?" she asked.

"To get away."

His quiet whisper tickled her ear. She giggled and pressed her body into his. "I like that. I like that very much."

"I thought you would."

"But won't they go ballistic when they find we're not around, especially you?"

His lips traced the line of her jaw. She trembled in his strong arms and closed her eyes. It was time. It was time she told him she didn't just want him sexually. It was time to tell him how she really felt. She loved him. She loved him with all her heart.

"Max, I want to tell you something. I realized something. I think I'm—"

He silenced her with a kiss. "Shhh. It can wait."

"But I want to tell you. I need to tell you."

The corners of his eyes crinkled. "And I've got something to ask of you."

Her heart soared. "What?"

"Not until we reach the top." He gestured towards the mountain peak.

She groaned. "I don't want to go another inch. I don't think I can."

"Of course you can. I have a surprise for you at

the top."

Chloe imagined a sparkling diamond ring, a symbol of his commitment to her and only to her. That was what she wanted. She wanted what every woman wanted—love and marriage and all the bells and whistles that came with it.

But it couldn't possibly be a ring. Why would it be a ring? They hadn't talked love yet. And then there was the wacky, crazy, annoying show they were both committed to. No, she was really daydreaming now.

"Maximilian, what are you talking about?"

He chuckled. "I don't think you've ever called me that. I can't remember the last time anyone actually called me that. I sort of like it."

"Well, I'd call you by your complete name, but I can't remember it," Chloe told him. "It must've been horrible for you."

"How so?"

"As a little boy. Trying to remember that ridiculously long name."

"It was. That's why I decided eons ago I wanted to be called Max."

"How old were you?"

"Five. I stood up to my mother and father and announced I didn't want to be called Maximilian or Alexander or anything else. I was Max."

She smiled at the vision of Max as a little boy with huge blue eyes and curly black hair. "It suits you."

"Thanks." He offered his hand. "Come on. It's not that far. You'll love it at the top. Trust me."

She took his hand, and warmth spiraled through her as his skin touched hers. A simple touch and she melted. She had found her soul mate—she was positive of it. She wished she could stop time. She never wanted the morning to end. She wanted to stay in the desert with him forever and ever and ever. She never wanted to go back to the mansion or to the women who believed he was their property.

"So, can you explain the origins of your name?" she asked as they resumed their climb.

"You mean the entire ridiculous thing: Prince Maximilian Alexander Henry Tarleton Radborne?" She nodded. He sighed. "Family names. Every Radborne male has the name Alexander. My brother's name is Rafferty Alexander William Tarleton Radborne."

"Does your brother go by Rafferty?"

Max burst into laughter. "He loathes his name. He hates it. I have to admit I'm happy I didn't get his name. He refuses to respond if we call him that. He goes by Rafe." A mischievous smile curved his lips. "Of course, my sister and I love to call him by his full name just to piss him off."

Chloe joined in his laughter. "Sisters and brothers are so mean to each other."

"You too?"

She nodded, jumping over a small hole. "Yeah. My sisters and I have a love/hate relationship. Mostly love, but a little hate thrown in there."

"What's your middle name? I'm sure you don't have fifty names like I do. It's very American to only have a first name, a middle name and a last name. I think royalty could learn a thing or two from Americans."

Chloe wrinkled her nose. She detested her second name, and she wasn't a big fan of her first name either. "You don't really want to hear it."

"I do."

She shook her head. "No. I think I'll take that one to my grave."

"Ah, come on, I shared my atrocious name with you."

"It's not exactly a secret, Max."

He shrugged. "Even so."

"Okay, okay. I'll tell you, but you have to promise you'll never tell anyone. Not even Jules knows it."

"It can't be that bad."

She stopped, dropped his hand, and narrowed her eyes. "I'm serious."

Max held up his arms and surrendered. "I promise."

"And you can't laugh."

His eyes rounded. "I promise. Honestly, I cross my heart. I won't tell a soul, and I won't laugh."

"I know you're lying."

"I'm most definitely not. That last thing I want to do is make you mad at me."

His sparkling blue eyes gave him away. He might not tell, but he'd certainly laugh.

She shook her head and placed her hands on her hips. "No. I don't think I'll tell you."

"Ah, come on."

"No."

"I wouldn't do anything to betray your trust. It means a lot to me."

"It's just a name."

"Well, if it's just a name, you shouldn't have any trouble telling me."

She gave up. It was impossible to resist him. He was so darn cute standing in front of her, his blue eyes begging her to reveal her horrid little secret.

"Bertrine. I'm named after both my grandmas." She pointed accusingly at him. "And don't you dare laugh. You promised!"

"Bertrine?" he repeated. His voice shook with laughter. She had to give him credit. He was doing a very good job at holding it in. "Bertrine?"

"Yes," she snapped irritably. "See. I knew I shouldn't have told you."

"Chloe Bertrine Tanner."

She grimaced. "Oh, please don't repeat it. It

sounds horrible."

"Chloe Bertrine Tanner."

"Stop it!"

"It's not so bad."

"It's horrible, and you know it."

"Do your grandmas know how much you hate their names?"

"No. I never wanted to hurt their feelings. They're both gone now, and I miss them dreadfully. They were wonderful ladies; they couldn't help having less than attractive names."

"Okay, I have to agree with you about the Bertrine. But I rather like Chloe."

"I guess it's not so bad. You get used to it. Supposedly it's making a big comeback."

Max reached for her hand. "Shall we continue? We're going to miss the sunrise." He looked over her shoulder at the distant horizon. "Actually, I think we already did."

She happily took his hand again. She could care less about the sunrise. She was just enjoying being with him—that was all that mattered to her.

"I suppose you'll continue the name tradition with your sons?"

"It's expected. At least Alexander."

"That's a nice name," she commented as they rounded the last curve in the path. They were finally at the top. Scottsdale, Phoenix, and an array of other suburbs stretched out below them. A fine example of urban sprawl, but the view of the desert was still lovely. Early morning sunlight streamed across the rocky terrain of the purple-hued McDowells.

He turned to face her. "I never really thought about children until recently." The heat of his gaze seared her insides.

Her heart stopped beating. "Oh?" she squeaked.

"Not until I met you. Now that's all I can think of."

She swallowed hard. Her heart started beating again, wildly slamming against her ribcage. "Really?"

"Yes." He cupped her face in his hands. "Do you ever think about children, Chloe?"

She had never given much thought to having children. She had a slew of nieces and nephews. She adored each one and never forgot to send a card and gift on birthdays. But to have a child of her very own? No, she'd never dwelled on it much. But now she could see her children, Max's and hers, playing and dancing before her eyes. They'd have Max's blue eyes and his fantastic smile, with those irresistible dimples. Oh, what little princes and princesses they would be! They would be the little darlings of the media. Watching out for them, protecting them, loving them would be a full-time job.

The domestic thoughts startled her. Had she really changed so much in the past few weeks? She'd never thought about settling down and starting a family before. Her career had always been most important to her. She'd pushed everything else aside, especially after having her heart broken a few too many times. Her high-school boyfriend Greg had only been the start of many disastrous relationships, each one leaving her more battered and bitter than before.

And now Max stood before her in the haze of an Arizona sunrise, promising her the world in his blue-blue eyes. And she wanted to believe. She wanted so badly to believe the fairy tale could be reality. But did she dare to? Not a moment before, she had been more than willing to confess her love for Max, but now she wasn't so sure. Suddenly she was frightened. She was frightened of giving her heart to him and having it abused and shattered again.

"Chloe?"

She focused on his handsome face. His smile

was warm and tender, his blue eyes soft and loving. She loved him. She did. And she was about to risk everything for that love.

"Chloe? Are you okay?" He reached for her, and she stepped into his embrace. "Darling?"

She squeezed her eyes shut and leaned against him, wrapping her arms about him and holding him close. "What are we doing, Max?"

"What do you mean?"

"This. Everything. I don't know. I only know it breaks my heart to see you with those other women."

"But I don't care for them as I do for you. You know that. You have to know that."

She nodded. She knew. But it didn't change their situation. Nothing would.

Except her confession. "I have something to tell you."

"Will you help me with something first?"

"All right."

"I wanted a moment alone with you this morning because we're changing the show a bit."

"What do you mean? What changes are you talking about?"

"You have to promise me you won't get mad."

A warning alarm sounded in her head. This couldn't be good. It certainly didn't sound good. "Okay, what is it?"

"I thought it would be a great twist to the show if you'd help me choose where I'm going to take the final four contestants."

She stared at him in complete and total shock. What? What was he talking about? Wasn't it horrible enough she had to live night and day in the same mansion as all his prospective brides? Wasn't it tortuous enough for her to watch him court those beauties and act as though each one could possibly be his princess, the queen of his country, and the mother of his precious heirs?

"Excuse me? Could you repeat that?" Chloe gripped the soft fabric of his shirt.

He grinned, that adorable, lopsided, amazing grin. "I think you heard me. Isn't it a fabulous idea? Toni and the producers loved it. It gives you more camera exposure and adds a new dimension to the show. Most of all, it gives us a chance to be together."

"But we won't be alone. The cameras will be with us all the time."

"Does that matter?"

She gaped at him. "Of course it does! I don't want our relationship unfolding in front of the crew and in front of the entire world!"

Max's grin vanished. "I thought you'd be pleased I found a way for us to be together."

Chloe disentangled herself from him and walked a few paces away. She needed some breathing space. She needed to set herself apart from the magnetic Prince Max.

Hot anger flowed through her. She had been about to express her love for him. About to open her heart to him; about to risk everything for the love she felt for him. She'd been so positive he felt the same. How could his expressive blue eyes lie to her? Did he truly only care about the blasted show? Was that all she meant to him? A ratings booster?

His hand touched her shoulder as a tear slid down her cheek. She pulled away from him and walked the rest of the way up the mountain until she was standing at its very peak. The view below was breathtaking, but she couldn't appreciate its stunning uniqueness because of the overwhelming pain pounding inside her bruised heart.

Max came up behind her. She felt his presence, and she wanted to turn into his arms. She wished he would sweep her off her feet and carry her away to their happily-ever-after. But she knew that wasn't going to happen. Not now. Not ever.

"What did I do? I thought I was helping."

"How? How can you possibly think that?" she asked quietly. She hugged herself and wished she'd refused his invitation. She wished she'd just stayed in bed, buried her feelings, and went on as if nothing existed between them.

"It's a way for us to be together."

Chloe continued to stare down at the Valley of the Sun. She didn't want to face him. She couldn't face him. He'd see the devastation in her eyes. He'd see how much she hurt, and she couldn't have him see her that way. She just couldn't.

"I'm not interested." She tried to keep her voice steady, but she heard the tremble in her words. She knew he did as well. "Tell them I'm not going to do it."

"I thought you'd be happy."

Was he that dense?

"I thought you'd be thrilled to spend time with me."

How could he not see? How could he not understand? Spending time like that with him would be worse than what she was going through now. Choosing places to take the *Courting His Royal Highness* contestants on his dates? Was he crazy?

"Please talk to me."

"I'm not doing it, Max."

Silence filled the small space between them.

"Chloe?" he pleaded softly.

"I want to go back down. Now." She took a couple deep breaths before turning around to face him. "I'm not doing this."

Max looked away from her, focusing on something unknown over her shoulder. "That's not possible."

"Why?"

"Because they've already written it into the

show. You'll be getting the new information today."

She was flabbergasted. "But I haven't given my consent."

"It doesn't matter, Chloe. This is how it works. You signed on and they can do anything they want. Reality shows are like that."

"And I suppose you're the expert?"

"No. I'm not. But I know what we signed. Do you?"

She had to admit she hadn't read the contract very thoroughly. She'd been so overjoyed to have an actual job in the entertainment business, she'd signed rather quickly on the dotted line.

Well, now she'd learned her lesson. She'd never do that again. If only she'd known she was signing over her heart. She wondered if the contract stated anything about that—relationships on set, or something. It probably did. She wouldn't be surprised.

"It was my idea."

"Why didn't you talk to me?" she asked. The warm rays of the morning sun couldn't chase away the chills in her body. "Why?"

His eye gazed into hers, and she saw the pain in the blue depths. She knew he hadn't meant to hurt her. He'd only wanted to give them more time together, to explore the feelings between them. But how could they do that in front of the camera lens? She didn't want that; how could he? And in the end, they couldn't be together anyway. He had to pick one of remaining girls to be his bride.

"I'm sorry. I thought I was doing something good for us."

"Us?" She laughed, a cold and bitter laugh. "There is no *us*."

"I don't believe that."

"You have to."

"I don't."

Chloe tore her gaze from his. She knew she'd lose all hope of keeping her composure if she continued to look into his eyes. "You can't have everything, Maximilian," she whispered sadly. "You can't have me."

"I can!" he exploded.

Chloe jumped as he grabbed her roughly by the arms and drew her hard against him. "Let me go!" she cried.

"No. I'm not going to let you out of my arms until we've had a chance to clear the air."

"Clear the air? What are you talking about?"

"You and me. I don't give a damn about this show. Not now. Not after meeting you. You have to believe me."

She struggled against him, unwilling to look into his intense eyes, unwilling to yield to him. "Let me go!"

"No! Not until you understand. Not until I've explained. I was going to wait until the end, but I see that's not possible. You have to know now. I see that now. I can't play with your emotions."

"What end are you talking about? You're not making any sense?"

"Stop struggling and calm down so we can talk like two rational adults!"

But Chloe had no intention of calming down or of staying in his arms. She had no intention of listening to him any longer. She needed to run from him before she broke down and cried in his arms and confessed everything in her heart.

"If you care for me, you'll let me go," she hissed angrily, pushing at his chest with the palms of her hands. "You're forcing me to stay here. You're not giving me a choice. Is that what you want?"

He shook his head. "I want you to choose to stay with me."

"No."

"I don't want to let you go until we've talked."

"About what? About this ludicrous idea of yours? I'm not them!" She frantically gestured in the direction of the mansion, where the women waited in anticipation for him to return. "I'm not going to compete for your affections. I'm not going to do it."

"You don't have to compete. You already—"

"No! No! No!" She pushed at him again, but he held strong. She stomped on his feet; he refused to loosen his grip. "I care for you, and you know that. How can you take those feelings and manipulate them like this by putting me in this situation? How? Explain it to me if you can."

"I thought I was doing the right thing for both of us."

"Well, this is not the right thing. It's horrible. It's awful. It'll make things worse."

"How?"

"Because I love you!" Chloe shouted. She slapped a hand over her mouth in shocked amazement. She hadn't meant to reveal that bit of information. She hadn't planned on him ever knowing how she truly felt. Not after what had happened.

He released her immediately. Chloe practically fell to the ground. She regained her footing and backed away from him, refusing to look at him. She was afraid of what she'd see on his face, in his eyes. He didn't love her. He didn't love her at all. She'd been stupid to think that he did. Why would a man like Max love her? She was nothing special. She was nothing special at all.

"Chloe, please stop. We need to talk."

She shook her head. Tears blurred her eyes. "Forget I said it. Please forget I said it. I didn't mean it."

"You didn't?"

"I'm sorry I said it."

"Don't say that, Chloe."

She stared at the ground and miserably drew her toe through the sandy soil. It had started out as such a beautiful morning. She wished she could go back. Only an hour. An hour would change everything.

"Chloe, I have something to say to you, but I can't say it when you're looking at the ground. Look at me. It's important."

"I don't want to hear it," she sobbed.

"Yes, I think you do."

"Nothing you can say will make me feel better."

"I think I can make you feel better."

Chloe heard the smile in his voice, but she refused to look up. What could he possibly be smiling about? This was the most mortifying moment of her entire life.

"Look at me." His husky voice filled the air around her, enveloping her in a cocoon of warmth. "Look at me. Hear what I have to say."

There was something in his voice. She couldn't put her finger on it, but something was different— something that gave her hope maybe her outburst had not been in vain.

"There you two are! We've been looking high and low for you both. You gave us quite a fright."

Chloe spun around and was surprised to find Eric Von Stratton coming around the curve in the path. She heard Max mumble a few expletives under his breath. Von Stratton's appearance was most definitely not part of Max's plan.

"How are you today, Miss Tanner?" he asked, touching the brim of his baseball cap.

"Just fine. And you?" She'd never seen him in anything but a suit. He looked completely different in a black running suit and cap.

"I'd be a whole lot better if Max had given me specifics about his plans this morning."

"I don't have to tell you everything, Eric," Max snapped. "When I need an hour for myself, I need an hour. I don't need to explain anything."

Eric Von Stratton stopped in the middle of the crooked path and shook his head at his boss and friend. "Someone did not wake on the right side of the bed this morning. It is my duty to know your schedule, Max. You're family would never forgive me if I let something happen to you."

"What's going to happen to me in the desert?" Max asked.

"A diamondback could bite you."

"You have an answer for everything," Max grumbled.

Chloe smothered a smile. Even in her present state—near a complete emotional breakdown—she couldn't help but find the exchange amusing. Their interaction always was.

"That's my job." Mr. Von Stratton pulled out his black scheduling book and flipped it open. "Now we have to talk about the day's events."

"I'm sort of busy right now."

"I was just leaving," Chloe said. She walked around Von Stratton, refusing to look at Max.

"But we haven't finished our conversation, Chloe."

"I think we have, Your Royal Highness. I think we have." She finally looked back over her shoulder, forced a sunny smile, and waved at Max and his diligent assistant.

Chloe started to run as soon as she rounded the bend in the path, around the shadowed side of the McDowell's and out of Max's sight, and she didn't stop until she reached the privacy of her bedroom. Once there, she promptly threw herself across the bed and allowed herself a long cry that lasted until she fell into an exhausted sleep.

Chapter Twelve

"That could've gone went a whole lot better," Max moaned after Chloe disappeared from view. "Thanks a lot, Eric. Remind me to thank you sometime for ruining my life."

"Don't be so dramatic. Your life is far from ruined." Eric pushed his glasses up the bridge of his nose. "What are you talking about? What exactly did I do that was so horrible?"

"You interrupted a very important conversation." Max slapped his thighs with the palms of his hands. "Damn! Damn! Damn!"

Eric tucked the schedule book under his arm and sat down on a nearby boulder. "Okay, spill. What's going on here?"

"She loves me."

"She loves you?"

"Yeah."

"She actually said that?"

Max nodded. "And I was about to tell her I feel the same—before you showed up uninvited."

"You're quite angry, aren't you?"

"That's an understatement, my old friend. I'm angry with you, with me, with her, with this entire situation. I should've never done this. This show was a huge mistake. Colossal, actually."

"I did warn you; however, it wasn't because I thought you'd fall in love with Miss Tanner. I like her. I like her a lot, and I think she would make an excellent Romalian princess."

"You do?"

"I do. I also know your family would absolutely

adore her."

"I hurt her. I hurt her real bad. If only you'd seen the look on her face, the pain in her eyes. I've really messed this one up. I wanted to surprise her. It was the wrong decision."

"How did you hurt her?"

"I thought I was helping. I suggested to the producers that Chloe be even more involved by helping me pick out the perfect dating event for the last four candidates."

"And you thought *that* was helping?" Eric started to laugh. His eye sparkled at Max. "How so? Especially after what happened between you two. People have to be blind not to see the sexual tension between you and Miss Tanner. It must be torture for her to do this crazy show, knowing she can't show her true feelings about you or be alone with you or have a chance at being your wife. You've really done it this time, Max. You're in over your head, and you're drowning."

Max dragged fingers through his hair. He couldn't forget the sadness in her luminous eyes. It was hard to push aside the image of her tears and the emotional trembling of her lovely voice. He'd broken her heart. He knew that and regretted it with his entire being.

He never wanted to cause Chloe pain. He never wanted her to be alone or feel sad or unloved or betrayed. But something had gone horribly wrong. He'd been so thrilled at the concept of spending more time with her, even if it was in front of the cameras and hundreds, eventually millions, of people. He thought she'd feel the same. He'd been wrong, so horribly wrong. He'd had a plan. And that had been just one small part of it. It had seemed so perfect. And now it was crumbling to pieces around him.

But she did love him. Her passionate words echoed through and through his mind over and over again. Chloe loved him. She'd admitted it. Her feelings went deeper than mere physical attraction. She loved him.

And he returned her love tenfold. He'd planned on telling her, but now he wondered if she'd even listen to him. She was so angry, so bitter, so hurt.

She probably wouldn't speak to him again unless the script called for it. And even then, it wouldn't be her speaking—it would be her character, the beautiful hostess helping the bachelor prince select a bride. The mask and armor would be on full force. He wouldn't be able to reach her.

"So, should we go over the schedule for today?" Eric asked, opening the black book, pen at the ready.

"For once be my friend, you blockhead! I don't need an assistant!" Max roared. "Give me some advice. I need advice from my best friend."

Eric looked up at Max and offered him a sympathetic smile. "I feel for you, Max, I truly do. But I'm not sure what advice I can possibly give you. I don't have much experience with women. I'm far too busy managing your life—and we need to talk about that, by the way. I do know you love her. I've never seen you so affected by a woman. You never take your eyes off of her when she's in the room. You never stop talking about her. I still can't believe this all started as a one-night stand."

"I fell in love with her then, Eric. I never believed in love at first sight, but I do now. It does happen. It happened to me and to Chloe. And now I have to find a way to make it right. I have to give her the happily-ever-after she deserves."

"The fairytale ending you both deserve."

Max smiled sadly. "Thanks."

"I mean it. You can be the most exasperating friend and boss, but you're a great guy and you deserve happiness. If Chloe is your happiness, then you should do anything and everything to be with her."

"That's your advice?" Max asked.

Eric nodded. "Most definitely."

"I have a plan."

"Is it better than the idiotic one you just mentioned?"

"Better. Actually, this fiasco was but one small part of the bigger plan."

"Wonderful. You'll have to tell me all about it, but it'll have to wait until this evening. The schedule's packed for the day. We won't have a chance to discuss it unless you want to fill me in on the way back to the mansion."

"I'll fill you in. It's a great plan, better than great. I only hope Chloe loves me enough to forgive me for what I'm about to do and understand why I had to do it."

Eric's eyes widened. He looked worried. "I'm not sure I like the sound of this, Max. It sounds like it has disaster written all over it. And more heartache for Miss Tanner. And possibly for you."

"I don't think so. She loves me. She only needs me to tell her I love her back. Then all this hurt and anger will melt away. I know it will. She'll forgive me. She has to."

"What are you scheming?"

"The proposal of a lifetime." Max smiled. "I'm going to sweep her off her feet and carry her off into the sunset on a white horse, just like in the fairy tales."

"And how are you going to pull that off?"

Max's smile widened. "That's what I'm going to tell you, dear friend. And I was hoping you could help me out."

"I'm not agreeing to anything until I've been informed about this plan."

"Very well."

And Max told his friend all about the plan he'd

discussed over the phone with Toni. And Eric had to admit it wasn't such a bad idea—but its success depended on Chloe. It all depended on how much she loved Max, and on whether she would forgive him his secrets.

Chapter Thirteen

Chloe was late for another meeting with the production team and Max. She didn't know if she could take much more of this. The last couple of weeks had been excruciating. She was emotionally, physically, and mentally exhausted. Keeping her feelings hidden from everyone was the most challenging and difficult thing she'd ever done. She was truly acting. She deserved an Emmy. Actually, she believed her acting to be Oscar-worthy.

But, thankfully, there was now only one week left of *Courting His Royal Highness*. Max had narrowed it down to the final two, Elizabeth from England and Ingrid from Norway. He would select his bride at the end of the week. Chloe was relieved. Only five more days, and it would be over. She would finally be rid of the thorn in her side: Max. And she wouldn't have to be with him every day.

She was definitely looking forward to some peace and solitude. She'd miss him so very much, but she couldn't do this much longer without having a breakdown. She was close to it now.

Only five more days. She could do it. And then she was taking a hiatus to Minnesota, where she would stay through the New Year. The producers had suggested she keep a low profile while the show aired on the EVE Network, and her family's farm in rural Minnesota seemed the perfect escape. She planned on stopping in L.A. to pick up Domino—then home. She missed her family. She missed the farm.

She was even looking forward to the seclusion.

Chloe had started to wonder if maybe she didn't enjoy being in the spotlight as much as she'd originally thought. But she knew it was ignorant of her to make judgments based on this one experience. After all, she happened to be madly in love with her co-star. That affected things quite a bit, and it wouldn't always happen. This was a unique situation.

Courting His Royal Highness had debuted last week to rave reviews. It was the newest hit and the must-see show of the season. Americans were addicted, and the rest of the world had tuned in as well. EVE had purposely arranged it so *Courting His Royal Highness* would be seen all across Europe, and it was the headliner in Romalia every day.

Chloe had phoned Julia to ask what she thought, and her friend couldn't stop raving about it. Julia kept saying how fabulous she looked and that Max was sooooo incredibly handsome. He took her breath away, and she hoped with all her heart things would work out between them. She didn't believe Max would actually have to marry one of his choices if he wasn't in love with her. The executives at EVE couldn't possibly hold him to that. In Julia's opinion, it would be beyond cruel.

Chloe, on the other hand, believed less and less in the possibility of a happy ending for Max and her. Max looked very happy with his choices and didn't seem to be giving her a second thought, despite the fact she'd confessed her deepest secret to him. How could he forget what she'd said? People didn't say "I love you" casually. At least *she* didn't. Maybe Max did. She could count on one hand how many times she'd told a man she loved him.

As she descended off the last step and onto the cool tile of the spacious foyer, she was mortified to see Ingrid and Elizabeth coming in the front door. Both were dressed in designer workout outfits, one

Amy Hahn

in pink and the other in purple, and both giggled like teenage girls.

Chloe froze. She didn't want to talk to either of them. She wanted to scratch out their pretty eyes and claw out the gorgeous strands of their perfect hair. How could anyone compete with them? She'd always been happy with her looks, but they were *perfect*. Every woman who had vied for the coveted position as Max's princess had been perfect.

Ingrid and Elizabeth were Max's final choices. One would be his bride.

"Hello, Miss Tanner!" Ingrid cried. She waved and rushed over, blonde ponytail bouncing. "It's so nice to see you."

"You see me every day," Chloe said through a forced smile and clenched teeth.

"Yes, but it's usually in front of a dozen eyes." Elizabeth giggled. "We're so excited about this week. Do you know where Prince Max is taking us on our final dates?"

Chloe shook her head. She didn't know at the moment, but she was about to find out. The meeting's agenda focused on the preparations for the final week.

"You must know. You can tell us. We promise we won't tell a soul." Ingrid winked. She fit the stereotype of a Scandinavian woman: blonde, blue-eyed and long-legged. Her blue eyes were as mesmerizing and magnetic as those of the man she hoped to claim as her husband. They'd produce breathtaking children. Chloe's heart ached.

"I can assure you I don't know. Sometimes I'm as much in the dark as you."

Elizabeth's eyes widened in surprise. "Truly? That doesn't seem right." She had auburn hair, possessed the greenest eyes Chloe had ever seen, and she had a smile like sunshine. That was the only way to explain it. Max had described it that way

184

when he'd discussed the attributes of each contestant.

"I also wouldn't tell you if I did know," Chloe said softly. "I'd love to chat, but I have to run. I'm extremely late for a morning meeting." She looked down at her watch for emphasis and hoped they'd let her hurry on by without further questioning. "Goodbye. Have a pleasant day. I'll see you this evening."

"Miss Tanner, do you think he'll choose me?" Ingrid asked. Her eyes shone. "I like him so much."

"What about me? I like him too, and there's definite attraction between us," Elizabeth interjected.

Ingrid glared at Elizabeth. "With me too."

Chloe forced herself not to roll her eyes in exasperation. "I'm sure Prince Max feels attracted to each of you. You're the final two out of fifteen. But he has to decide which one of you he has the strongest feelings for. Choosing a bride is a big deal and can't be taken lightly. Be thankful you've made it this far."

"Oh, we are!" they exclaimed in unison. "We're so happy. One of us will be a princess. Can you imagine that? A princess!"

The ache in Chloe's heart grew five times bigger. "I'm glad you're happy."

She wished she could feel the same. But all she felt was misery every single day. And she wanted out. She wanted to get away from everyone, but mostly Max. She didn't want to feel the intensity of his blue eyes as he watched from across the room. She didn't want to see him courting, embracing, and kissing other women. She wanted to be away from it all. The show couldn't end fast enough.

"Isn't he the dreamiest man you've ever seen in your life?" Elizabeth asked. "I've never met anyone so handsome and gentlemanly in my whole life. He truly is a prince."

"That's what his pedigree says," Chloe remarked. She couldn't keep the sarcasm from her voice. Talk about torture. "I have to go."

"Bye, Miss Tanner."

"Have a good meeting."

Chloe hurried in the opposite direction, out the back door, across the pool area, and to the guest cottage where the meeting was being held. She took a deep breath and tried not to think of what surprises awaited her beyond the door. She had a very bad feeling about this meeting, and she didn't want to attend. For a split second, she considered turning around and hightailing it back to her bedroom. But she couldn't do that. She was so close to finishing this job, to honoring her contract.

"You can do it," she whispered softly. She lightly rapped her knuckles on the door.

"Is that our hostess?" Mr. Parker's irritated voice boomed angrily through the door.

"Yes," she replied, wincing at the croaking sound of her voice.

"Come in. Come in. We've been waiting for you. We can't have a meeting without our lovely hostess."

Chloe took another deep breath and pushed the door open. Mr. Parker and several members of his production team sat around a large rectangular table. Max and Eric Von Stratton were also there, and both smiled warmly as she entered. She acknowledged them with a quick nod before sliding into an empty seat.

"I'm sorry. I truly am."

"Oversleeping again, Miss Tanner?" Mr. Parker asked.

"A late start."

"I need another cup of coffee." His assistant jumped from her chair, grabbed his empty mug, and filled it to the brim. "You know I hate to have an empty cup."

"Yes, Mr. Parker." She set it before him on the table and offered him an apologetic smile, but the smile faded when he didn't thank her. Chloe felt sorry for the girl. She waited on him hand and foot and he hardly took notice of her at all—that was, until his coffee cup was empty.

"We can start, now that Miss Tanner has decided to grace our lives with her presence." Mr. Parker took a long drink of his freshly brewed coffee. "Actors," he snickered softly.

Chloe reddened. She hoped she didn't have too many directors like Jack Parker in her future. She wanted to chop his head off as much as she wanted to claw out the too-perfect hair of Ingrid and Elizabeth.

"Good morning, Chloe."

Chloe's eyes met Max's across the table. "Good morning."

"We've been discussing what's going to happen during the final week."

She nodded. "Yes, I read the agenda."

Mr. Parker hooted. "Well, isn't that a first. Usually you choose to read the agenda at the meeting or after. I think you're improving—though your punctuality could still use a little work."

"That's enough, Mr. Parker. Shouldn't we get on with this meeting so we can attack the rest of the day?" asked Eric Von Stratton. He frowned with disapproval at Mr. Parker.

Chloe tossed a thankful smile in his direction, and Von Stratton smiled back. She liked Max's sidekick. She admired his loyalty to Max and felt as if he'd started to look out for her best interests over the past couple of weeks. It was nice to be protected; she could get used to someone taking care of her.

"That's an excellent idea, Mr. Von Stratton." Mr. Parker picked up his agenda sheet and began to rattle off the week's priorities.

It didn't take long for Chloe's mind to drift. She only bothered to listen in meetings when things directly related to her, which happened very little. Max was always involved, as were the contestants, but she was usually in the background.

As the meeting continued, she tried not to focus her attention on Max. She slathered a blueberry bagel with cream cheese and politely asked Mr. Parker's doe-eyed assistant for a coffee. The people at the table continued to talk about agenda items she only vaguely understood. She supposed it would be in her best interest to listen and learn, but she didn't really want to. The whole conversation seemed so meaningless, so trivial. She had bigger issues on her mind, and she didn't have a committee to solve them. Was there such a thing as a committee for mending broken hearts? That was the meeting she needed to attend.

"Now that we've taken care of the major issues, let's move to the last item on our list. Chloe, we need you for this."

Chloe quickly swallowed the piece of bagel in her mouth and dabbed the corners of her mouth with a napkin. "And what is that, Mr. Parker?"

"The choosing of the ring."

She swallowed again. She wasn't sure she had heard correctly. "What did you say?" she whispered hoarsely.

"The ring. You're going to help the prince choose a ring for his bride."

Chloe reached for a glass of water and took a long drink. Her hand shook, and the bracelets on her arm rattled against the colored glass. This couldn't be happening! She was going to choose the ring? How could Max ask her to do this? But he wasn't asking her—the show's director was. Still, it felt like Max was behind this. Another betrayal. Another way to torture her. She wanted to look at him, but she forced herself to keep her gaze on Mr. Parker.

"The ring? But shouldn't Prince Max do that?"

"He's selected three, but he'd like your opinion."

"My opinion?"

"Yes." Mr. Parker turned to his terrified assistant. "Get the rings."

"Yes, Mr. Parker." The assistant reached underneath her chair and pulled out a small black velvet bag. "Here they are, sir."

Chloe still refused to look at Max. Feeling the heat of his gaze on her, she wanted to die. She simply wanted to die. She'd thought things couldn't get any worse, but this had to be the icing on the cake or the nail in the coffin—she wasn't sure which cliché she'd use to describe her feelings at that moment. Probably the one about the final nail in the coffin. Yep, that sounded about right. Dying. She definitely felt like dying.

"I don't think I want to do this," she admitted softly as the assistant untied the bag and pulled out three blue boxes. "I think Prince Max should choose on his own."

"I can't, Chloe."

She looked across the table into Max's blue eyes, and her heart stopped beating. The tenderness in his eyes took her breath away.

"I need your help."

"But I can't do this. I can't do this."

"You can. Choose the one you like the best, Chloe."

"The cameras aren't rolling, Miss Tanner," Eric Von Stratton assured her softly. "We promise." He turned to Mr. Parker. "Right, Mr. Parker? You promised. No cameras, hidden or otherwise."

"Yes. No cameras. We agreed," snapped Parker. "But I want to be on the record as saying I think that's a bad idea."

"Noted." Von Stratton turned back to Chloe. "Go ahead. Choose one."

Chloe glanced around the table. Everyone nodded, affirming his statement. They smiled encouragingly at her, each and every person at the table, and she felt an overwhelming feeling of love. She was startled by it. She'd been so focused on getting away, leaving because of her feelings for Max; she'd forgotten how wonderful the people she worked with were. Even Mr. Parker had his moments. He wasn't always brash and insensitive; in fact, she'd learned a lot from his tutelage. Over the course of the last five weeks, they'd become like family to her.

She laughed, trying to act as if she hardly cared about choosing the ring Max's fiancée would wear upon her finger. "Yeah. No big deal. They're only rings, right?"

Heads nodded in unison, and looks were exchanged. They almost looked as if they all shared an amazing secret, a secret she knew nothing about. But that was ridiculous. Julia had always criticized her about being paranoid.

"What's going on here?" No one responded. She turned to Max. "Max?"

"I know this is difficult. And I'm sorry to ask it of you, but could you please help me one last time?"

The people around the table faded into nothing. She only had eyes for Max. He filled the entire room. His blue eyes, his gentle smile. His hands covered hers, and she wanted to weep with joy. His touch felt so incredibly good; she never wanted to be without it again.

"This is hard for me, a nearly impossible task," she whispered.

Max nodded. "I understand. I'm not trying to hurt you."

Her fingers curled about his. "How can I choose

a ring for you to give someone else? How can I do it?"
A sob caught in her throat. She closed her eyes
briefly, praying for composure. She was surprised
she wasn't angrier with him, but she couldn't be. She
was tired of being mad at him, so very tired. She just
wanted it to be over.

"Choose the ring you like best. Do it for me. This
last time. One more favor."

One could argue she'd done too many favors for
him, but she was finished with fighting. She nodded
and pulled her hands from his.

"Miss Tanner?"

Chloe nodded at the assistant, who opened the
shimmering boxes. Three rings blinked back at her.
She gasped in appreciation of each one's unique
beauty.

"Oh, my goodness," she sighed. She couldn't help
but smile. The diamonds glimmered brilliantly in
the light. One was a round stone with a gold band,
the second a marquis shape with a white and gold
band, and the last was the loveliest piece of jewelry
she'd ever seen. She touched it lightly with her
fingers. It was exactly the ring she would've selected:
a square-cut diamond mounted on a thick platinum
band, it was simple and elegant and yet extravagant
and oh so very royal. She fell in love with the ring. It
was the ring from her imagination. It was the ring
she'd always hoped for.

"This one." She looked up at Max and smiled.
Tears pricked the corners of her eyes. "This is the
ring you should give your bride-to-be. It's perfect. It's
exactly the one I'd pick to be mine."

"That's the one I thought you'd choose." Max
smiled *her* smile, the one he reserved only for her,
and Chloe longed to throw herself into his arms and
confess her love all over again.

He loved her, didn't he? He had to. There was no
other way to interpret the deep tenderness in his

blue eyes.

"That's a wrap!" shouted Mr. Parker. He quickly downed the remainder of his coffee. "Mystery solved. We're going with the square-cut diamond. Everyone may leave now; get back to work. We've got a big week planned."

A dozen people rocketed from their seats and bolted for the door, filing out in a chattering stream and leaving Max and Chloe and Eric Von Stratton in the room.

"A tasteful choice, Miss Tanner."

"Thank you, Mr. Von Stratton."

"We should go, Max. We've got a lot to plan."

"Thank you for choosing."

"It wasn't as hard as I thought." She watched as he closed the lids on the boxes and tucked the treasures back into the black bag. "It truly is the most beautiful thing I've ever seen."

Max leaned forward and kissed her cheek. "You are the most beautiful thing I've ever laid eyes on. Diamonds can't compare. Nothing can compare."

She closed her eyes and breathed in his scent. Gosh, he smelled good. She wanted to remember that soapy freshness for as long as she lived. His breath caressed her cheek. His lips were light and gentle. She wished for more time with him; she wanted to be with him forever. A tear slipped free, zigzagging down her cheek, and he wiped it away with his thumb.

"Don't cry."

"Why not? There is so much to cry about."

"You're going to have everything you've ever dreamed of. I promise you that."

She opened her eyes and looked directly into his. "How can you promise me that when all I want is you?"

Von Stratton politely cleared his throat. "I'm sorry to break this up, but we have to go. We have to go now. Things to plan. Things to plan."

Max drew away from her. She felt cold without him near.

"Goodbye, Chloe."

"Goodbye, Max."

And she knew it was their final goodbye. It was over. Despite his romantic promises. It was over. At last. For good.

It was the saddest moment of her entire life.

Chapter Fourteen

"You look beautiful, Chloe. You're going to knock their socks off."

Chloe smiled sadly into the mirror. She wrapped a string of pearls about her neck and wished she could stop the trembling in her fingers. The *Courting His Royal Highness* makeup and wardrobe staff had done an excellent job. She looked like a princess. She looked better than she'd ever looked in her entire life, except for portraying Queen Mab at the EVE Halloween Ball. She would probably never look this lovely again.

"I'd like a minute by myself," she pleaded softly to the bubbling assistant Linda, an adorable college intern who thought *Courting His Royal Highness* was the best gig in the entire world. She idolized Chloe and was goggle-eyed over the charming Prince Max.

"No problem. I can't believe tonight's the final night. I'm so bummed. This job was awesome. I'm so lucky I got to do it."

"We were lucky to have you on board. You do magic with makeup and hair," Chloe complimented sincerely. "I've never looked better."

Linda flushed with pride. "Thanks, Chloe. I'll tell everyone you'll be down in a few minutes."

Chloe smiled at her. "Try to keep Mr. Parker from having a heart attack while waiting for me. And hide the coffee."

Linda giggled as she set down the brush on the small vanity. "I'm really going to miss you," she whispered, trying to smile through the tears that filled her eyes. "I hope EVE will hire me. I really need a job. I really want a job in Hollywood."

Chloe reached over and squeezed her hand. "I'll be a reference for you."

Linda glowed. "Truly?"

Chloe nodded. "Truly."

"You're the best boss in the world!" cried Linda, startling Chloe by throwing her arms about her and hugging tightly.

Chloe hugged her back. "You're the best assistant I could ever have. I'll not forget you."

Linda pulled back. "Maybe I'll work for you someday."

"Maybe."

"I just know you're going to be big. This show is going to skyrocket you to stardom."

At one time, being a famous movie star had been all Chloe ever wanted. A career in the movies was what she'd dreamed of.

But now things were different. She only wanted the man downstairs. She only wanted the prince who would select his princess tonight. And she would not be chosen. She was not a choice. She had never been a choice.

"Go. I promise I won't be too late." She forced a shaky smile. "Only typically late."

"Fashionably late," Linda teased.

Chloe laughed. "Yes, fashionably late. That's fits me exactly."

Linda gave Chloe another hug before leaving the room. She closed the door softly, leaving Chloe alone with her thoughts and a tidal wave of emotions that threatened to drown her.

Chloe looked back at her reflection. She did look lovely—very royal-like. Her dark hair was piled on top of her head, secured by a tiny tiara of pearls and diamonds. It was very tiny, hardly the type of crown a true princess would wear. She'd been shocked when Linda showed it to her and refused it initially, but that was what the director wanted her to wear. So that was what she'd do.

Dark tendrils of her hair tumbled down about her neck and shoulders in soft curls. Dangling diamond and pearl earrings danced on her ears, and the four-stranded pearl necklace was gorgeous. More exquisite than any piece of jewelry she'd ever owned, it looped elegantly about her long neck. She touched it lightly with shaking fingertips.

"I can't do this. How can I do this?" she whispered at her reflection.

Tonight she had to give him away. Officially. Finally.

Her throat tightened, and she swallowed a sob. Max was the love of her life. She didn't know how she would ever live without him. And yet she had to. She had to move on with her life. Without him. Alone.

Some other woman, Ingrid or Elizabeth, would exchange vows of love and honor and fidelity with him. One of them would have the honor of being his wife, of gazing into his amazing blue eyes every morning, of being loved every day, of curling in his arms every night.

"I can't think about that now. I can't. I'll fall apart if I do. Tomorrow I can think about him, about us, about what might have been. But tonight I have a job to do. Tonight I have to hold it together. I have to be brave. I can't let others see how my heart is shattered, how my life is in shambles."

Chloe smoothed the satin of her dress. She loved the dress. Long and elegant, with a high empire waist and full skirt, it swooshed about her as she moved. She felt as though she'd stepped off the pages of a fairy tale. And the best part about the dress was that the soft blue satin fabric seemed to replicate the exact shade of Max's eyes.

She stood, grabbing the matching wrap off the back of the chair. She draped it about her shoulders and took one last look at herself in the mirror.

"Chloe, you'll put on the best performance of your entire life," she told herself. "You will. No one will know you're in love with Max. No one. Even Max himself will wonder if he actually heard you say that you loved him."

The words made her feel better, more confident. She squared her shoulders and took a deep breath. She decided she needed to keep telling herself over and over again tonight that her goal was to make sure no one know of her feelings for Max. It was a challenge, but she could do it. She had to. And it was going to work—she knew it was.

Twenty minutes later, she'd changed her mind. She didn't feel so brave or so confident. Being in the presence of Max, his bachelorette choices, and surrounded by the entire production crew rattled her already frayed nerves. The scrutiny of the camera lens didn't help either.

It wasn't going to work. Most definitely. Most certainly. All of America and the world would be able to see her love for Max. There was no way she could hide it; attempting to do so was a hopeless task.

Max looked so handsome—every woman's dream. He took her breath away. Just gazing upon him gave her so much joy. She wanted to run across the patio and wrap her arms about him and hold him close to her heart. She wanted to claim him as her own in front of everyone. She wanted Ingrid and Elizabeth to know he didn't belong to either one of them. She wanted to make it clear he was hers and hers alone.

But she wasn't brave enough. Even when his eyes caught hers and he smiled the smile that was only meant for her. She hated herself for it. She hated that she didn't have the backbone, the nerve, the guts to throw caution to the wind and take a chance on love.

Who cared about EVE or the production crew or Toni back in Los Angeles? Did they really matter? And was her career that important? Wouldn't there be other opportunities? Did a person truly only have one chance in Hollywood? That couldn't be true. Life was full of second chances.

"We'll be ready to roll in ten minutes! Everyone take their places!" barked Mr. Parker.

It suddenly occurred to Chloe that she didn't know Max's choice. Wasn't she supposed to know? She'd known everything else, including Max's final two selections. And the ring. After all, she'd selected it herself.

She hurried up to the high-strung director. "Excuse me, Mr. Parker, but I don't know which girl Max is choosing. Shouldn't I know?"

Mr. Parker shook his head. "No. It was decided that you weren't supposed to know. It adds more suspense and drama that way, if even you are in the dark."

"So, you all know and I don't. That doesn't seem right. After all, I am the hostess and part of team. Besides, I helped Max with all his previous choices."

Mr. Parker took a long sip of coffee. He smiled kindly. "Sorry. Upper management made the decision."

Chloe was positive she detected a mischievous twinkle in his eyes. And Mr. Parker's eyes didn't normally twinkle. They just didn't; he wasn't that type of guy. He was serious about his work and didn't have time for humor.

Chloe didn't like this one little bit. Something was going on, and she wanted to find out what. She'd never been particularly found of surprises.

"I demand to know what's going on."

"I need you to take your place next to Max. We have to get this show rolling. No time. No time." He tapped his wristwatch with the bottom of his coffee mug. "I'm on a tight schedule here. Very tight."

Max appeared at Chloe's side and placed a hand on her arm. "Is something wrong?"

The heat of his bare hand seared her skin, and she stepped away from him. "No. Nothing. Not really. I just don't understand why I don't know your choice."

He dimpled at her. "Don't you like surprises?"

She glanced away. "That all depends on what type of surprise."

"Would you two please take your places? We can't start filming until both of you are in place," snapped Mr. Parker irritably. "I need more coffee." He handed his empty cup to his ever-present assistant. "I don't know which is worse, royalty or actors. And I don't have time to figure out which."

"He is an impossible man," Chloe hissed under her breath.

Max chuckled. "He's very intense, but Jack's a good guy." He touched her arm again. "Chloe, I wish you wouldn't look so sad."

"I'm not sad." She moved her arm an inch to the left, just enough so his fingers slipped off. Heat still radiated up and down her arm. She hated the effect he had on her. No, she loved it. But she had to forget how she felt when he touched her. "I just want to finish this show so I can get on with my life."

"Without me," Max said quietly.

"Without you," she whispered. "Can we please get on with this?" She walked away from him, holding her head high and trying not to notice how wonderful he looked in the midnight suit and blue silk waistcoat and matching blue tie.

He followed closely at her heels. "I don't want it to end. Ever."

"Why? Because you enjoy flirtatious romps with beautiful women?"

He grasped her elbow. "Only with one beautiful woman." The husky gentleness of his voice caused the skin on the back of her neck to prickle.

She tugged her elbow roughly out of his hand without stopping. She was not about to fall prey to his charms again.

This was it—she was in the home stretch. Only a few more hours of this torture, and then it would be all over.

But deep down, she didn't want it to be over. Ever. She wanted it to last and last and last, because at least she was with him now. That wasn't always going to be the case.

They walked on a path of crushed rock, moving away from the lighted patio and towards the moonlit backyard. A full moon hung high in the night sky, and thousands of stars blinked like diamonds in the darkness. The shadows of the McDowell Mountains were etched against the inky sky.

"Is it Ingrid or Elizabeth?" she asked, ducking under the branches of a low-hanging desert willow. The tree was illuminated from trunk to branch tips with tiny white lights. The entire garden was decorated in the romantic white illumination, making it a more enchanting setting for a marriage proposal from a prince.

"Stop. Stop this."

"Stop what?" She halted and spun around, slamming her face very ungracefully into his chest.

"This. Denying what we feel."

She rubbed the tip of her nose ruefully and glared up at him. "This is a broken record. I'm tired of talking. I'm so tired of doing this. I'm exhausted." And she was. She felt as

though she could curl up in bed and sleep for the next year. That wasn't an exaggeration.

"Chloe."

She loved the husky way he spoke her name. No one spoke her name like Max did—no one in the whole world. Tears blurred her eyes. She turned her head to the side and looked away from him, unable to gaze into his eyes.

He grabbed her shoulders. "I'm tired of talking as well. How about if we simply feel." He pulled her to him and kissed her cheek, her forehead, the line of her jaw, and the corner of her mouth.

She remained stiff in his arms, refusing to melt into his tempting embrace. "Don't. Don't make this more horrible than it already is," she pleaded hoarsely. "I'm beginning to think your whole purpose in life is to torture me mercilessly, ruthlessly, heartlessly."

"Not true. Not true at all. The farthest from the truth," he murmured as he continued to kiss her. His lips were warm, and the feathery touch of his kisses on the curve of her ear and the slope of her neck caused her to tremble. His fingers curled with possessive gentleness on her shoulders. As his body shifted closer, he whispered her name over and over again until at last she couldn't resist him. She turned her head, and when his lips covered hers, she sobbed against his mouth. She wrapped her arms around him and kissed him back with intense emotion.

"Trust me," he murmured in her ear.

She collapsed completely against him and buried her face against his broad chest. "Even you can't have everything you want. Do you even want me?"

She felt his smile against her hair. "You are all I have ever wanted or will ever want. I promise you that."

"Max? Chloe?" It was Eric Von Stratton.

"Trust me?"

201

Chloe smiled sadly and walked away from him. "We're over here, Mr. Von Stratton."

He appeared out of the shadows, smiling warmly at Chloe. "You look quite lovely tonight, Miss Tanner. A vision of loveliness."

She offered him an over-exaggerated curtsy. "Thank you very much, Mr. Von Stratton."

His eyes sparked merrily behind his round glasses. "They're ready for you. Good luck."

Max offered her his arm. "Shall we?"

Chloe smoothed the front of her dress, flipped a few wayward curls over her shoulder, and blinked a couple times to clear the tears from her eyes.

"Ready?"

"I'm ready. As ready as I'll ever be." She placed her hand on his forearm. He stepped forward, and she clasped his arm tightly. "I wish you happiness, Max. I want you to know that. To always know that."

"And you. That's what I want for you. Love, health, and happiness."

"Hurry up, you two. They're waiting." Eric Von Stratton literally pushed them forward; Chloe almost tripped over the hem of her dress. "Tonight is the beginning of great things," he whispered behind them. "Great, wonderful, extraordinary things."

Maybe for Max and his new bride—but not for me. I feel as if I'm going to the gallows.

They stepped out together into the view of the cameras and the glare of the lights. She smiled brightly into the camera and read the lines she was supposed to deliver with practiced ease. She'd never had a problem memorizing dialogue—she was a quick study. She briefly summarized the final week's events and introduced Elizabeth and Ingrid again to the audience. Images and video would be added after the shooting finished and the editing had begun. Footage from Max's last dates with the women would be shown, along with Max's comments about each girl and Elizabeth and Ingrid's comments about him.

She managed to do it all in one take. That was how badly, how very desperately she wanted to be done with *Courting His Royal Highness*. The elation of six weeks ago had vanished, and in its place, only pain existed. The already popular show—according to an overzealous Julia—was going to launch her into the career of her dreams. All the things she'd ever wished for and prayed for were about to come true.

But were they truly? She couldn't help but wonder if she'd ever be happy without Max in her life. She'd have to watch from afar, just like the rest of the world. She'd read about him and his family in magazines, and every now and then catch glimpses of him on the television.

Chloe somehow managed to introduce Max to the cameras without her voice cracking or tears streaming down her cheeks. She stepped into the background and let him take center stage, watching as Max talked to his audience. He was an old pro. He had the royal smile on, the one he reserved for his adoring public. He was animated and charismatic and he shined. Elizabeth and Ingrid waited in breathless anticipation for him to make his choice. They held hands and looked utterly breathtaking in their long black gowns.

"And so, it has finally come to this. I have chosen the woman I want to be my bride." Max paused. He glanced over at Elizabeth and Ingrid, smiling at each one. They smiled back.

"Both are lovely, wonderful, talented women. I was lucky to meet each of them. I consider myself very fortunate to have met so many amazing women. There were fifteen originally, and now there are two."

Chloe stood silently, barely breathing.

Max looked back into the camera. "I feel I should be honest. My choice was not hard to make. It was perhaps the easiest choice I've ever had to make. My heart made it for me. And I'm glad it did. I'm so very glad."

Elizabeth and Ingrid giggled.

Chloe wanted to die.

And then Max turned his attention on Chloe. And he dimpled. His thousand-watt smile beamed only at her, only for her. It was *her* smile. His eyes looked directly into hers, and Chloe's heart started to race. Her hands flew to her chest, splaying across her rapidly beating heart. Something was happening.

He looked back at the camera. "Love found me. I never thought it was possible. I never imagined I would find love, especially on a reality television show. But I did. I found it. Or it found me." He smiled sardonically. "I guess the world's Prince Charming found his fairytale princess." He focused on Elizabeth and Ingrid. "I hate to break any hearts. I hate to cause any pain. I'm sorry. I apologize to both of you. I apologize because I choose neither one of you."

Chloe gasped in unison with Elizabeth and Ingrid. Their mouths opened wide in astonishment. In any other setting, it might have been comical. But not here. Not now. Not under these circumstances. Chloe held her breath. What type of game was Max playing? What was going on here?

She looked around and noticed that no one else seemed shocked. Eric Von Stratton grinned from ear to ear, as did every member of the camera and production crew. And even Mr. Parker smiled. This was not a surprise to them. They had known all along that Max was going to do this.

"So, you'll marry no one?" Elizabeth asked.

"I don't know. That's up to someone else."

"Who?" asked Ingrid.

Max turned to face Chloe. And his heart was in his eyes. "Chloe. My future is in her hands."

She started breathing again. Her legs wobbled; she nearly lost her balance. Happiness spread through her like a raging river. This was beyond her wildest hopes. This was beyond all her dreams. How on earth had he managed this?

Max rushed to her, grasping her hands in his and sinking to one knee. "I love you, Chloe Tanner. I love you with all my heart. Do you still feel the same for me?"

A sob tore free from her throat. She cupped his face in her hands, and her fingers lovingly traced the handsome lines of his face. She supposed she should be angry with him for keeping her in the dark about this, for the deception. But she didn't feel angry with him at all. It was too beautiful a moment. And she knew he'd put a lot of work into making this special for her.

"You know I do," she whispered. "I love you. For always."

He reached into the pocket of his jacket and pulled out a velvet box. He flipped open the lid, and the ring she'd chosen sparkled at her. Tears slipped through her lashes and cascaded freely down her cheeks. Her entire body shook as he took her left hand in his and poised the ring at the end of her third finger.

"Marry me. Be my partner for life. Be my bride. Be my princess."

Max slid the exquisite ring onto her finger. It was a perfect fit. The square-cut diamond caught the light, flashing so brilliantly it nearly blinded her. No other piece of jewelry would ever be more precious than that ring upon her finger. It symbolized so much.

He stood and folded her in his arms. She

encircled her arms about his neck and smiled up at him. She'd never been so happy.

"This is what you meant."

He quirked an eyebrow at her. "Whatever do you mean?"

She laughed. It felt good to laugh. "About trusting you."

"What did I tell you?"

"That you always get your way."

He nodded and kissed the tip of her nose. "That's right. Prince Max always gets his way. Of course, it did have to be your choice. I may have not gotten my way."

"Would you have accepted my rejection of your proposal?" she asked.

"Never. You belong to me, and I belong to you. Our not being together is not an option. It never was."

He lowered his head and kissed her. The kiss was so long and so passionate that when he pulled away, she had to clutch tightly to him for fear of fainting dead away. She flushed in embarrassment. The eyes of the cast and crew were on them. The eyes of millions would witness that kiss, unless Mr. Parker decided it should be edited out; of course, he wouldn't to that. It was too good. Much, much too good. She could vouch for that.

She was rather pleased to be on the receiving end of that spectacular kiss.

"I think I fell in love with you the first time I met you," Max murmured. He stroked a curl away from her face. "But I didn't realize it right away. Now, I'm definitely a believer in love at first sight."

"Me too." She touched his cheek with the back of her hand.

"Me too."

He kissed her again.

"Cut!" shouted Mr. Parker. "That's a wrap!"

Chloe smiled against Max's lips. "Should we have him be in charge of our wedding?"

"I don't think we have a choice. Remember, our wedding will be a major production for EVE. I think Mr. Parker is the director."

She groaned. "Heaven help us."

Max kissed her again. Members of the cast and crew started clapping and hooting their appreciation. He dipped her low and deepened the kiss, causing the hollering and applause to increase in volume.

And Chloe knew without a doubt she was the happiest woman on the entire planet. Happy endings did happen. She'd found her Prince Charming. She hoped the millions of single women of the world wouldn't give up on theirs. Maybe *Courting His Royal Highness* would prove that to them.

It had proven it to her. Beyond a doubt.

Thank you for purchasing
this Wild Rose Press publication.
For other wonderful stories of romance,
please visit our on-line bookstore at
http://www.thewildrosepress.com.

For questions or more information,
contact us at info@thewildrosepress.com.

The Wild Rose Press
http://www.thewildrosepress.com

Other Champagne titles you might enjoy:

HOW MUCH YOU WANT TO BET? by Melissa Blue Neil never thought a game of pool could change the course of her life, but when she plays against Gibland Winifred the Third she knows she's liable to lose both the game and her heart.

CATASTROPHE by Sharon Buchbinder. Cats! Twenty-three of them! They and their owner are being evicted, and their handsome neighbor doesn't want to lose any of them, especially the curly-haired, curvaceous woman. Can they come up with a rescue plan?

HIBISCUS BAY by Debby Allen. Picture love on a sun-drenched white sand beach surrounded by hibiscus-covered cliffs, with your yacht anchored in a blue Mediterranean Sea.

TASMANIAN RAINBOW by Pinkie Paranya. A concert violinist grapples with remote ranch life, intrigue and the mystery of a missing diary, the peril of a flood in which all could be lost, and the undeniable attraction of the man who would do anything to protect his son.

THREE'S THE CHARM by Ellen Dye. Rachel vowed never to speak to her ex-husband again. But her beloved horse falls ill and Heath is the only vet within three counties of West Virginia mountains, and some vows need to be broken.

THE CHRISTMAS CURSE by Marianne Arkins. Dressed as Mrs. Claus, Molly meets the man of her dreams, who turns out to be a nightmare, in a broken-down elevator. Her Christmas Curse is right on track.

SEE MEGAN RUN by Melissa Blue. City-successful Megan goes home to the boonies to save her childhood home but finds she must not only agree to stay for her mother's wedding but also deal with the man left behind when she hitchhiked out 12 years ago.